I0610652

DID YOU BOO HOPALONG CASSIDY?

Richard Baran

A Mouse Gate Adventure

Mouse Gate™.
1103 Middlecreek
Friendswood, Texas 77546
281-992-3131   281-482-5390 Fax
www.totalrecallpress.com

All rights reserved. Except as permitted under the United States Copyright Act of 1976, No part of this publication may be reproduced, stored in a retrieval system, or transmitted in any form or by any means electronic or mechanical or by photocopying, recording, or otherwise without prior permission of the publisher. Exclusive worldwide content publication / distribution by TotalRecall Publications, Inc.

Copyright © 2019 by: Richard Baran
Edited by William R. "Will" Barshop
Copy Editors, Carol Fredrickson, Julie Laren,
Lisa Puck and Joseph "Bucky" Baran
www.buckbaran.com
All rights reserved

ISBN: 978-1-59095-328-0
UPC: 6-43977-43282-7

Printed in the United States of America with simultaneous printings in Australia, Canada, and United Kingdom.

FIRST EDITION
1   2   3   4   5   6   7   8   9   10

This is a work of fiction. The characters, names, events, views, and subject matter of this book are either the author's imagination or are used fictitiously. Any similarity or resemblance to any real people, real situations or actual events is purely coincidental and not intended to portray any person, place, or event in a false, disparaging or negative light. The scanning, uploading and distribution of this book via the Internet or via any other means without the permission of the publisher is illegal and punishable by law. Please purchase only authorized electronic editions, and do not participate in or encourage electronic piracy of copyrighted materials. Your support of the author's rights is appreciated.

To: A. M. D. G.

Author Richard Baran

Richard Baran holds a doctorate and two masters' degrees besides his bachelor's in business. A Navy veteran, he taught and coached for forty years at the secondary school and collegiate levels. His first novel and award winning, *The Jacket* was published by Total Recall Press in 2014. Subsequent novels, *Where Have all the Go-Go's Gone? Book 1; Wehn Will They Ever Learn? (Where Have all the Go-Go's Gone?) Book 2, The Dutchman's Gift, Shutter Bug* and *Heroes and Idols* were published by TotalRecall Publications Other publishing credits include, *Coaching Football's Polypotent Offense*, a coaching text, a short story, *That Ain't No Walleye* and several dozen articles in professional business, education and coaching journals. He and his grammar school sweetheart, Carol Ann have eighteen grandchildren and they divide their year between Franklin Park, Illinois; Phoenix, Arizona, and Minocqua, Wisconsin.

Visit www.richardbaran.com for more information.

About The Book

A pair of magical miniature cowboy boots reported to have belonged to the old western movie and television hero, Hopalong Cassidy find their way into the hands of twelve year old twins, Hanky and Elsa Jane Goodson. The boots and twins experience cattle rustlers, being kidnapped, fighting off a giant rattle snake and being saved by Hopalong Cassidy and a group of old cowboys who look familiar to Hanky and his sister known as, E Jee.

Hopalong Cassidy

From Wikipedia, the free encyclopedia

This article is about the fictional character. For the American

football player, see Howard Cassady.

Hopalong Takes Command, illustration by Frank Schoonover for the 1905 story "The Fight at Buckskin"

Hop-along Cassidy is a fictional cowboy hero created in 1904 by the author Clarence E. Mulford, who wrote a series of popular short stories and many novels based on the character.

In his early writings, Mulford portrayed the character as rude, dangerous, and rough-talking. From 1935, the character—as played by movie actor William Boyd in films adapted from Mulford's books—was transformed into a clean-cut hero. Sixty-six popular films appeared, only a few of which relied on Mulford's stories. Mulford later revised and republished his works to be more consistent with the character's screen persona.

Film history

Poster for the 1935 Hopalong Cassidy film *The Eagle's Brood*

As portrayed on the screen, white-haired Bill "Hopalong" Cassidy was usually clad strikingly in black (including his hat, an exception to the western film stereotype that only villains wore black hats). He was reserved and well spoken, with a sense of fair play. He was often called upon to intercede when dishonest characters took advantage of honest citizens. "Hoppy" and his white horse, Topper, usually traveled through the west with two companions— one young and trouble-prone with a weakness for damsels in distress, the other older, comically awkward and outspoken.[1]

The juvenile lead was successsively played by James Ellison, Russell Hayden, George Reeves, and Rand Brooks. George Hayes (later to become known as "Gabby" Hayes) originally played Cassidy's grizzled sidekick, Windy Halliday. After Hayes left the series because of a salary dispute with producer Harry Sherman, he was replaced by the comedian Britt Wood as Speedy McGinnis and finally by the veteran movie comedian Andy Clyde as California Carlson. Clyde, the most durable of the sidekicks, remained with the series until it ended. A few actors of future prominence appeared in Cassidy films, notably Robert Mitchum, who appeared in seven films at the beginning of his career.

The 66 Hopalong Cassidy pictures were filmed by independent producers who released the films through the studios. The first "Hoppies," as the films were known, were distributed by Paramount Pictures to favorable returns, and United Artists was the distributor after Paramount. They were noted for fast action and outdoor photography (usually by Russell Harlan). Harry Sherman wanted to make more ambitious movies and tried to cancel the Cassidy series, but popular demand forced Sherman back into production, this time for United Artists. Sherman gave up the series in 1944, but William Boyd wanted to keep it going. To do this, he gambled his future on Hopalong Cassidy, mortgaging most of what he owned to buy the character rights from Mulford and the backlog of movies from Sherman.

In the first film, Hopalong Cassidy (then spelled "Hop-along") got his name after being shot in the leg. Hopalong's "drink of choice" was the nonalcoholic sarsaparilla.

Television and radio

Boyd resumed production[2] in 1946, on lower budgets, and continued through 1948, when "B" westerns were being phased out. Boyd thought Hopalong Cassidy might have a future in television, spent $350,000 to obtain the rights to his old films,[2] and approached the fledgling NBC network. The initial broadcasts were so successful that NBC could not wait for a television series to be produced and edited the feature films to broadcast length.[3] On June 24, 1949, *Hopalong Cassidy* became the first network Western television series.

The success of the television series made Boyd a star.[2] The Mutual Broadcasting System began broadcasting a radio version, with Andy Clyde (later George MacMichael on Walter Brennan's

ABC sitcom *The Real McCoys*) as the sidekick, in January 1950; at the end of September, the show moved to CBS Radio, where it ran until 1952.[4]

The series and character were so popular that Hopalong Cassidy was featured on the cover of national magazines such as *Look*, *Life*, and *Time*.[2] Boyd earned millions as Hopalong ($800,000 in 1950 alone),[2] mostly from merchandise licensing and endorsement deals. In 1950, Hopalong Cassidy was featured on the first lunchbox to bear an image, causing sales for Aladdin Industries to jump from 50,000 to 600,000 in one year. In stores, more than 100 companies in 1950 manufactured $70 million of Hopalong Cassidy products,[2] including children's dinnerware, pillows, roller skates, soap, wrist-watches, and jackknives.[5]

There was a new demand for Hopalong Cassidy features in movie theaters, and Boyd licensed reissue distributor Film Classics to make new film prints and advertising accessories. Another 1950 enterprise saw the home-movie company Castle Films manufacturing condensed versions of the Paramount films for 16 mm and 8 mm film projectors; they were sold through 1966. Also, in January 1950 Dan Spiegel began to draw a syndicated comic strip with scripts by Royal King Cole; the strip lasted until 1955.[6][7]

Boyd began work on a separate series of half-hour westerns made for television; Edgar Buchanan was his new sidekick, Red Connors (a character from the original stories and a few of the early films). The theme music for the television show was written by Nacio Herb Brown (music) and L. Wolfe Gilbert (lyrics). The show ranked number 7 in the 1949 Nielsen ratings, number 9 in the 1950-1951 season and number 28 in 1951-1952.[8] The success of the show and tie-ins inspired juvenile television westerns such as *The Range Rider, Tales of the Texas Rangers, Annie Oakley, The Gene Autry Show,* and *The Roy Rogers Show.*

After Boyd's death, his company devoted to Hopalong Cassidy, U.S. Television Office, retained control of Cassidy films but, by the mid-1960s, had withdrawn them from television and sales in home movie markets. This remained the situation until the mid-1990s, after many Cassidy fans had died, when the company made available to The Western Channel a package series of restored and cleaned negative-based prints of the films to cable TV. These remained available on that channel until 2000, when they were again withdrawn. Minimal effort was made at that time, nor has it been made since, to offer the films for home video, excepting two packages of compressed, multi-title Hopalong Cassidy anthology DVDs, the first requiring purchase of the entire TV series to obtain copies of about a dozen films and then, in 2014, a reissue of the remaining stock of these same DVD pressings combined with the remaining titles in a first-time pressing.

The TV series can be currently seen on Cozi TV.[9]

Hoppyland

On May 26, 1951, an amusement park named Hoppyland opened in the Venice section of Los Angeles. This was an expansion and retheming of Venice Lake Park[10] (opened the previous year) as Boyd became an investor. Standing on some 80 acres (320,000 m^2) it included a roller coaster, miniature railroads, pony rides, boat ride, Ferris wheel, carousel, and other thrill rides along with picnic grounds and recreational facilities. Despite Boyd's regular appearances as Hoppy at the park, it was not a success and shut down in 1954.[11]

In other media

Novels

Louis L'Amour wrote four Hopalong Cassidy novels, which are still in print. In 2005, author Susie Coffman published *Follow Your Stars*, new stories starring the character. In three of these stories, Coffman wrote the wife of actor William Boyd into the stories.

Comic books/comics strips

Fawcett Comics published a Hopalong Cassidy comic book one-shot in 1943,[12] followed by an ongoing series from 1946–1953,[13] when the company ceased publishing. DC Comics took over the title in 1954 with issue #86,[14] publishing it until issue #135, in 1959.[15]

Mirror Enterprises Syndicate[citation needed] distributed a Hopalong Cassidy comic strip starting in 1949; it was bought out by King Features in 1951, running until 1955.[citation needed] The strip was drawn by Dan Spiegle.

Record readers

Beginning in 1950, Capitol Records released a series of Hopalong Cassidy "record readers" featuring William Boyd and music by Billy May, produced by Alan W. Livingston.[16]

Music

The song "It's Beginning To Look A Lot Like Christmas" includes a reference to Hopalong boots as a holiday gift desired by children.

Museums

There have been museum displays of Hopalong Cassidy. The major display is at the Autry National Center at Griffith Park in Los Angeles, California. Fifteen miles east of Wichita, Kansas, at the Prairie Rose Chuckwagon Supper was the Hopalong Cassidy

Museum. The museum and its contents were auctioned on August 24, 2007, owing to the failure of its parent company, Wild West World.

DVD release

On June 16, 2009, Echo Bridge Home Entertainment released the Hopalong Cassidy Ultimate Collector's Edition, which included all 66 theatrical films on 14 DVDs, packed into a facsimile Hopalong Cassidy tin lunchbox.

On June 7, 2011, Timeless Media Group released *Hopalong Cassidy: The Complete Television Series* on DVD in Region 1.[17] The 6-disc set features all 52 episodes of the series restored and remastered.

Prologue

Hanky Goodson was in trouble. He always seemed to be in trouble; if not the cause, at least a part. As a shy twelve year old he knew there was security in numbers. In numbers, he could muster up the nerve to do things he would only otherwise dream of doing. Now he needed more than numbers. He needed a way out. So did his twin sister, E Jee. The problem was there appeared to be no way out; at least not one that had them tied up by a notorious cattle rustler and facing a Diamondback rattle snake that was longer than Hanky and E Jee combined.

Chapter 1

Hanky had one thing in his life that he cared about, his grandfather, Joseph "Bucky" Goodson, a retired Chicago firefighter. Actually, Hanky had two things he cared about. The second was his fascination and total enthrallment with his grandfather's memorabilia collection of an old time movie and television cowboy hero, Hopalong Cassidy. Grandpa Bucky, as he was referred to by Hanky and his sister, Elsa Jane, did one thing that no one else did for or to Hanky. Grandpa Bucky always listened.

Sharing in Hanky's hero worship of a long ago movie and television star was his twin sister, Elsa Jane, or *E Jee* as she was called by everyone except her mother.

When Elsa got excited everything out of her mouth contained a, "Gee" or "Gee Whiz" or "Gee Willickers or, when she was really worked up, "Jeepers creepers, domineepers." That was her trademark and everyone who knew her accepted that fact and, of course, calling her E Jee which infuriated her mother who was rumored to have written the rules on manners and proper etiquette.

"Your name is Elsa Jane," her mother would remind her when hearing a variation of the "Gee's" coming from her daughter. "E Jee sounds like some form of Oriental board game."

Elsa's mother, however, did drop the formality of a single name when she was upset with her daughter. Then a middle and Confirmation name joined the mix to show her displeasure. "Elsa Jane Gertrude Goodson," she would state with added emphasis being placed on each name as it was announced, each name approximately one octave higher than the next. An exclamation point capped off the end of her displeasure.

Hanky, on the other hand, was well versed with the use of exclamation points when being addressed by his parents, relatives, teachers and most adults in general. He didn't seem to care. His friends knew only one way to talk to him and that was through shouting.

Hanky and E Jee were twins only by birth, Hanky being born first. There was no physical resemblance between brother and sister. They were opposites like oil and water and both had but one mutual like in common, an almost cult like fascination with their Grandpa Bucky's collection of Hopalong Cassidy. Oil and water found a way to mix together whenever the twins found themselves at their Grandpa Bucky's house sneaking peeks at his collection of Hoppy memorabilia. No one was a bigger Hopalong Cassidy fan than Joseph "Bucky" Goodson. Not even Hopalong Cassidy.

Visiting and peeking happened quite often since their grandparents lived one block to the west of them in the octagon brick bungalow where Hanky's and E Jee's father, Donald, grew up. Hanky and E Jee had a short cut to their grandfather's house that shortened the distance there in half. The short cut came from the courtesy of the Olsen and Mitch families—with or without permission—as their houses lined up with Grandpa Bucky's. An alley, a narrow sidewalk cutting between two houses and their respective backyards, and one street had Hanky and E Jee at their grandparent's back door knocking and waiting impatiently for a glimpse of their grandfather's Hopalong Cassidy collection. They always used the back door. They knew that their grandmother allowed only who she referred to as company through the front door and into her parlor. She felt that parlor was a more formal name than front room.

Grandpa Bucky was a squat, stern man who parted his silver grey, wavy hair slightly to the right of center. He was no taller than five foot eight, that on his best day when wearing his dress shoes, a pair of black Navy issue oxfords that he kept spit shined and wrapped in tissue paper in the same box they came in when he mustered out of the service when he was twenty one. He was now on the downside of sixty, retired from the Chicago Fire Department for several years and a growing pain to his wife of over forty years, Virginia, his high school sweetheart and a former beauty pageant contestant who always came in second.

Virginia Magnusson was the daughter of a Norwegian carpenter and a stay-at-home, one hundred percent Italian mother, Angelina. There were no traces of Scandinavian blood in Virginia Magnusson. Her maiden name was the only indicator. She hated the cold Chicago winters and let everyone around her know that fact. Virginia Magnusson also closely resembled the long ago famous Italian movie star, Sophia Loren and she wasn't shy about reminding any onlooker, the reminder coming with several assorted profiles and smiles she had mastered from studying various fan magazine covers. Her grandchildren had no idea of who or what a Sophia Loren was. She loved everything about her grandchildren except their referring to her as, Gram Gini, their pronunciation dropping the last "I" from her name. "It makes me sound like the cheap liquor that permeates this family's history."

"Whadda you two want?" Grandpa Bucky would always ask when he saw his two grandchildren waiting at the door. His question sounded like a growl with a flesh tearing bite. Then he'd give his two grandchildren, the Double Mint Twins he called them, a smile. His head nodded for them to come in and to head toward the attic stairs. It was in the attic where Grandpa Bucky had built his den; an Oak English paneled study, the plans coming from "Handyman Magazine." The room was his pride and joy; his sanctuary and made the idle hours of his retirement palatable, helping him to keep his sanity and from being sucked under from boredom. His love of music also kept his head above water.

Grandpa Bucky loved woodworking and used that love and his skills to build his escape from reality. He detested the term, Golden Years and cursed it under his breath, referring to being a senior as nothing more than an old tarnished turd. To keep busy, he had hand cut all the oak wood in his den. With the assistance of a homemade miter box, he crafted the stiles and rails to give each oak panel a raised look. One wall in the den was complete with a built-in book case; left over cuts from the panels had made perfect laminate for the shelves. Grandpa Bucky also loved books. His favorites were any coffee table book that had to deal with fire engines, fire fighters and fires. Next came his love for ducks, that followed closely by his passion for fishing, northern Wisconsin seeming to call him every season from early spring to the Dog Days of summer until late autumn when snow flurries often joined him on the water. The fall of the year fascinate him when only a handful of leaves remained on the trees, the majority blanketing lake shorelines and forest floors in ankle deep fading colors that once glowed.

Grandpa Bucky had miniature speakers for his antiquated tape and CD player, his turntable for records sitting idle under a hard plastic cover. The speakers resembled fire trucks, a truck at each end of one shelf acting as book ends. He would spend hours behind the closed heavy oak door of his den listening to his music collection that Gram Gini couldn't stand. Few people, including his fire fighting buddies over the years, knew that they were in the company of an accomplished musician. Bucky Goodson could play sax, clarinet, piano, guitar, flute and some accordion. An exploding window hurling glass, metal debris and a ball of fire transformed three fingers on his right hand into unbending stumps. His injury didn't prevent him from fighting fires, but it did diminish his dexterity with his instruments limiting his playing to the bass guitar and composing music on a computerized system that cost him almost a half year's worth of pension.

"Don't you two ever get tired of old Hoppy?" he asked them, then smiling at their wide eyes and eagerness to get to the attic where one entire wall was a shrine set up to William Boyd. There was a collection of old movie posters, framed and spaced in chronological order. Two shelves were devoted to Hoppy memorabilia. Grandpa Bucky had one each of a camera, lunch box, coffee cup, milk bottle and a gun and holster set-- the guns cap pistols. On a single shelve stood a pair of worn Hopalong Cassidy cowboy boots. Those were his pride and joy and he relished telling his two grandchildren how, as a young boy their age, his mother tossed them into the garbage because, according to her, "You're going to grow up to be a cripple if you continue wearing those pieces of trash."

"But I went out and hunted them down," he said coating his story with the determination he used to find his boots. "I dug through every trash barrel and concrete garbage box in every alley in a four square block area of our neighborhood," he continued. Then he grinned. "Just goes to show you what happens when you really believe you can do something," he said. "Hoppy, as you know," he explained to Hanky and E Jee, "ain't trash because God don't make no trash." Grandpa Bucky sat down in his worn Lazy Boy longer, kicked out the worn, scuffed foot rest and eyed his two grandchildren. "Well," he said, a long pause following as he waited for either of the kids to respond.

It was Hanky who finally asked: "Grandpa, if you could have joined up with Hoppy back when you were a kid would you have?"

Grandpa Bucky's head went back and he let out a laugh. "Of course I would've, Hanky," he said, his eyes glowing. "But that would never have happened."

Two pairs of eyes asked.

"Because Hoppy was mad at me," he said, sounding almost sheepish and ashamed. "He shouldn't have been."

Two pairs of eyes continued to ask.

"Hoppy thought that I once booed him," he said, the word, boo shocking his listeners.

Two jaws dropped as their eyes continued to ask.

"I really didn't do it," he said, sincerity coating every word. "Heck, I'd never do anything like that; at least, not to Hoppy. He was my hero." He paused, reflecting. "But, I did know who did it."

Eyes still wide and jaws still down, their faces pleaded for more information

"I've never told this to anyone before, not even my parents or your Gram Gini. And, I trust that you two won't be a couple of blabber mouths when I explain to you what happened." He didn't wait for their reply and continued on.

"I was in the seventh grade," he started out. "I was an altar boy," he continued, looking proud. "For our dedication of serving Mass during the week and on Sundays and Holy Days of Obligation, the nuns and priests rewarded us altar boys by treating us to a trip to the circus." He closed his eyes and remembered it like it was yesterday and not over a half century ago. "We even got out of school to go," he continued, a smile forming. "Hopalong Cassidy was the star attraction at the circus back then," he continued. "Heck, he didn't do anything but ride his white horse, Topper, around the outside of the three circus rings in the middle of the Chicago Stadium." His head went from side to side a couple of times. "Man, but the Stadium was packed; had to be ten thousand kids there along with their parents. Us altar boys were chaperoned by the nuns and priests. The circus was fun; the aerial acts and the acrobats were exciting, the clowns funny. But, man oh man, when Hoppy came out, the kids went crazy. They were all jumping up and down. Some of them tried racing down the aisle to get closer to him, to hopefully touch him. What a sight. The Andy Frain ushers had all they could do to keep the kids under control. It was like a giant stampede or a rodeo with cowboys trying to hog-tie frisky calves." His head went from side to side again. "Hoppy was dressed in black riding his horse. Man, I never saw a horse look so white. Topper seemed to glow. Hoppy's guns glistened, the reflection off of his silver spurs almost made you go blind. Even his eyes and teeth sparkled. It was a sight to behold. Everyone including the parents, nuns and priest were in awe. The man was beyond cool. Us altar boys thought he was greater than God." Grandpa Bucky paused, closed his eyes and entered his dream world again. Then he broke into a big grin. "Then it happened. I couldn't believe it."

"Grandpa," E Jee interrupted a curiosity in her voice. "What's a Frainny usher?"

Grandpa Bucky stifled a laugh. "E Jee," he said, "an Andy Frain usher was like the security guards you see today. Back then, they wore blue, military style uniforms. Kind of like the Marines. They weren't like those bald headed oafs you see today with snarls on their faces and wearing orange vests like school crossing guards and having bad attitudes. No, Mam. Heck, Hoppy would've never put up with that." He paused and looked into the eyes of his captive audience. "The screaming had died down to where you could at least hear the person next to you, and then it happened."

What, the eyes asked?

"It was the loudest boo I ever heard."

"Really?" the eyes asked.

Grandpa Bucky's head went up and down slightly once. "About that same time, I had cupped my hands to my mouth to cover up a sneeze." He looked at his two grandchildren. "My hands dropped out of sight so fast they banged off my seat. "I know they were down and out of sight before that boo was finished, before anyone saw me." He gave another single nod. "I don't think anyone saw me. I know the nuns and priests didn't. I don't know if Hoppy even glanced in my direction. Then the kids all started screaming again; louder this time. I guess the kids got a second wind. Anyway, Hoppy finished his final circuit of the three circus rings, gave a final wave, doffed his black Stetson hat and disappeared through a big opening at one end of the Chicago Stadium." He let out a sigh. "Never saw him in person again."

"Jeepers creepers, domineepers," said E Jee, brushing the light brown bangs from one side of her forehead to the other several times as if her hand was a automobile windshield wiper.

Grandpa Bucky laughed out loud and slapped at his knees with both hands. "All we talked about when we got on the bus to take us back to school was that boo and who did it. We were all giggling and laughing. I was hoping no one had been looking at me when I sneezed. Surely they would have thought that my hands to my mouth were an indication that I had booed Hoppy. I didn't take any chances and continued laughing, playing dumb and acting innocent like the others. The priests and nuns weren't playing dumb. I could see they were mad and couldn't wait to get back to school to crucify the culprit. What I couldn't figure out was why everyone on the bus kept looking at me."

"Grandpa, you didn't?" said E Jee.

Grandpa Bucky's answer was swift. "Of course not," he said. He smiled at his granddaughter. "But, I knew who did and it wasn't me. Heck, I didn't want to join Jesus on the crucifix hanging on the wall in the front of our classroom for doing something so stupid." He paused surprised at how old emotions came back so intense. "I told the guys around me that it wasn't me. I had sneezed and my sneeze was over before the boo started. The guys kind of believed me." He paused. "But, the nuns didn't. They never believed anything we said unless it was something we memorized from our Baltimore Catechism or the spelling words we had to memorize for class." He glanced at his two grandchildren and realized they weren't going anywhere until they heard the rest of the story.

Bucky Goodson knew what being trapped meant. Trapped was one of many words he had memorized for Sister Mary Helen's notorious spelling tests. He was the only boy in the room whoever got a grade of "A" on those tests; all of the girls getting perfect scores on their papers. Bucky Goodson was trapped and he didn't need a spelling test to tell him that. There was nowhere to go, no place to hide. There was no escape from the box like habit of his teacher, Sister Mary Ming the Merciless as she was known by most of the kids in the class instead of her religious name, Sister Mary Helen. Sisters of the Blessed Virgin Mary showed only a face from under a white cap and box like hood covered by a black veil. A pair of hands poked out from the wide sleeves of the black habit they wore, a circle of large rosary beads around their waist the beads big enough to choke a horse the size of Hoppy's Topper. B.V.M.s were both respected and feared. Bucky didn't fear Sister Mary Helen because he knew that he could convince his favorite teacher of being innocent of most wrong doings. That he wasn't the one who booed Hopalong Cassidy at the circus didn't need his convincing skills. He didn't do it and he knew that Sister Mary Helen also knew. Sister Mary Helen, however, shocked him by not believing a word he said.

"Besides," Grandpa Bucky said to his audience of two, "Sister Mary Helen only believed the girls. Sister believed they didn't do it because they weren't altar boys and weren't even there.

Another reason was they were, of course, possible candidates for the convent. To strike the fear of the Lord into any one of them could possibly mean a lost candidate to wear a habit, never show their hair and walk around in black old lady shoes forever. We boys, on the other hand, were never to be trusted."

The memories continued to return. He remembered how the nuns envisioned every boy in the school as a consummate liar and only the use of the third degree could bring out the truth from any one of them; that, and requesting a meeting with parents at the convent during dinner hour.

"Honest, S'tir, I didn't do it," Bucky had said respectfully, trying to force his eyes to water up. Tears, he knew worked every time; well, almost every time. "I'd never boo Hoppy. He's my hero. He's a good guy. My parents even gave me a pair of his boots as a Christmas present."

"Did you boo Hopalong Cassidy?" Sister Mary Helen asked again. This time the question came out coated with a hiss, each word being annunciated in slow motion as if it were coming from his homework spelling list.

"No, S'tir," he said, his denial choked and actual tears forming in his innocent blue eyes. "I didn't boo anyone."

"Ever altar boy here at St. Ferdinand School has indicated that you were the culprit who brought shame and disgrace to our school and the altar boys," said the nun with the kind eyes that could change to sinister in a blink. "They saw your hands cupped to your mouth."

"I didn't do it," repeated Bucky, the tears flowing for real now and his nose beginning to run. "I was covering my mouth the way my parents told me to do when I sneezed." He sucked it in with a sniffle that sounded like he was cleaning out his lungs with the leaky air pump he used to fill the tires of his Schwinn bicycle. He watched the nun's right hand disappear into her habit and he knew that anything from a black jack to a comic book to a basketball could be pulled from beneath the black robes as if she were a magician. The only thing sinister that appeared was a Kleenex which she handed to him. He wiped his eyes, sniffled again and then blew his nose, the Kleenex turning useless and soggy in his hand.

"I'll talk to you later, Mister Goodson" said the nun, the look on her face stating that she had her criminal and was just putting the finishing touches on getting a confession from her prime suspect. "Now finish drying your eyes, go back to your seat and send me Donald Edward."

Sister Mary Helen addressed all of her students by first and middle names, never their last.

Bucky sniffled again, dabbed at his eyes with the soggy Kleenex trying to get rid of any evidence that a nun had made him cry, turned so Sister Mary Helen couldn't see the look of innocence plastered across his face and entered the room. Once the door clicked behind him, his demeanor changed from scared silly to a cocky, she-couldn't-scare-me look and gave the tall, gangly Donald Edward, also known as Mushy, a nod. "S'tir wants to see you in the hall."

The classroom was as silent as a tomb. Only a third of the boys in the room had been altar boys and had made the bus trip. That fact was immaterial. Someone would pay for booing Hopalong Cassidy even if they weren't an altar boy like Mushy who was walking home from school when the incident took place.

"Gee, Grandpa, are you joking with us?" asked E Jee, a coy smile on her impish face. "Did a teacher really make you cry?"

Grandpa Bucky kept a straight face and said: "Nah. I had something in my eye or my allergies were acting up. I don't know what." He paused giving each of them a serious look. "Now, I did know of a nun or two who made some of my pals cry." He tried not to smile. "I think one of them made my best friend, Tommy Fox, go number two in his pants."

"No way!" blurted out Hanky. He pushed his right hand over the top of his overgrown crew-cut that resembled the quills of a porcupine.

"Tell us about it, Grandpa?" pleaded E Jee covering up a case of the giggles.

"Can't do that," said Grandpa Bucky very serious. He didn't wait for their questions and he knew he would be bombarded by them. "Our Kid Code wouldn't allow that."

"Kid Code?" asked Hanky. "What's that, Grandpa; some kind of secret club, like a handshake?"

Grandpa Bucky remained serious. "Nah," he said, his mind going back to what he felt were the best times of his life. He felt his heart begin to glow. "The Kid Code was like the Articles of the Constitution of our United States of America," he started warmly. "It was our Ten Commandments; our Golden Rule. You did unto other kids as you would have them do unto you." He looked at Hanky and E Jee. "You two do that with your friends, don't you?"

Two nondescript looks flashed back at him. Grandpa Bucky

knowingly shook his head without being insulting or sympathetic or both to his grandchildren. Those were our rules," he continued, his eye brows going up as if asking, "Don't you and your friends have a set of rules you follow when you're playing or hanging out?" he asked. "Surely you have something."

Hanky and E Jee gave identical shrugs.

"Nothing, zero, zip, zilch," Grandpa Bucky rattled off. "Whadda you kids have, mob rule?"

E Jee giggled. "Oh, Grandpa, you're funny."

"We don't need no code, Grandpa," replied Hanky. "We know what she should or shouldn't do."

Grandpa Bucky flashed a smile back at them. "Learned all of that from your parents and teachers and the adult world, huh," he said.

"I guess," said Hanky.

"We didn't have any adults adding rules to our Kid Code," continued Grandpa Bucky. "Adults had their way of doing things and we had ours. We didn't want any adults. We had enough of that at home, at school, heck, adults were everywhere." His smile continued. "You poor kids get the life choked out of you by adults. We didn't have that. We didn't have any organized youth team coaches and umpires telling you what to do. None of that," he said explaining the law of the time; his time. "We didn't want parents at our games watching us and cheering, snooping around, asking questions, telling us what to do and all that dumb stuff. If someone was out at first base in one of our baseball or softball games, we settled it between us. We knew how to compromise even if we did yell a lot and get into a fight every now and then. Nobody pulled out a gun and shot at anybody back then. Not like what you guys hear about today. A neighbor's window might have gotten broken by a lousy throw, but we owned up to it and all chipped in to get the window fixed." He thought for a moment and then added, "Our Kid Code had an unwritten clause that stated that we would never rat on a friend unless, of course, it saved our butt from getting whacked by a parent—mostly our fathers. My cousin, Ronnie, never got hit by his father," he interjected. "It was his mother, my Aunt Estelle, who packed a wallop. My cousin feared his mother. That Kid Code you two are interested in, well that kept our lives on a pretty even keel. No police, no drugs and maybe a fight or two entered our lives back then. If there was a problem, we'd solve it; period, end of the Kid Code." He smiled lovingly at his two grandchildren. "Today, you kids have to carry those silly cell phones of yours for protection."

"They're called iPhones, Grandpa," said E Jee as she reached into her pocket to display her phone covered in a pink case.

"I got one too," said Hanky displaying his, a black case protecting the instrument. He held it up for his grandfather to see. "Pretty cool, huh, Grandpa"

"Yeah, cool," their grandfather repeated. "Must cost your poor father an arm and a leg to pay for those idiotic toys of yours," he continued.

"Mommy says they're for our safety," said E Jee displaying her phone with several slight twists of her wrist.

"If you had a Kid Code, you wouldn't need those contraptions," said their grandfather. "You'd have all the safety you would need." His last statement was emphatic and he stared at his grandchildren as if to insert a giant exclamation point after his words of, as he saw them, grandfatherly wisdom.

There unsure eyes were their reply.

His look at them grew more serious. "If you had a Kid Code, your parents wouldn't have to worry about your safety. The Kid Code would have you expecting the unexpected." Then Grandpa Bucky's look turned sad, almost looking despondent. "If I would have remembered the Kid Code and expected the unexpected when I was with the fire department, I wouldn't have had this." He held up his right hand. A constant numbness in his right hand that showed the slight signs of a tremor in his fingers were the result of his not expecting the unexpected. "Now, remember you two," he said, his voice even more serious than his look, "what is said in Grandpa's den stays in Grandpa's den."

Two heads nodded.

"Are you sure," he said as he leaned toward the book shelf alongside his chair and removed a small white box, the size a ring or a small piece of jewelry would come in. "I've got a gift for you two," he said removing the top of the box and a small square of cotton. He tipped the box on an angle for the twins to see.

"Tiny plastic cowboy boots," said Hanky not understanding.

"Gee, they're cute, Grandpa," said E Jee.

Their grandfather frowned. "They're neither cute nor plastic," he said sounding disappointed in the initial observation of his grandchildren. "They're real leather cowboy boots," he stated tipping the box on different angles then saying, "See."

The twins then saw their grandfather give them a look they never saw before and they both felt a chill. E Jee shifted her weight until she was almost glued to her brother's side.

"These boots are more than real," he continued, the look not changing. His eyes shifted back and forth. "They're magical," he said.

Excitement replaced the icy chill the two felt. They didn't know what to say.

Grandpa Bucky picked out one boot from the box and twisted it gently between his thumb and forefinger. "Here," he said, as he placed the boot in Hanky's palm. The other boot found its way into E Jee's hand. "These boots possess more than magic," he continued. He paused. "These boots once belonged to Hopalong Cassidy."

Two pairs of wide eyes responded.

"Those boots just might save your little hides one of these fine days," he said, his head going up and down ever so slowly. "Yep," he continued. "They just might come to your aid when you least expect it." His eyes twinkled. "Like expecting the unexpected," he said, his statement sounding like a prophecy.

"Grandpa," said Hanky as he felt the leather texture of the boot in his hand. "Are you funnin' us?"

Grandpa Bucky's head went from side to side, his look never changing. "Nope," he said. "Those boots were once worn by Hopalong Cassidy himself."   His eyes never left his grandchildren. "And, your grandpa ain't funnin' you either."

"But, they're so teeny weenie," said E Jee. "How could he…?"

Grandpa Bucky gave her a smile. "Did you miss what I said about those boots possessing magic?" he asked, his eyebrows rose as he waited for a reply from either of his grandchildren.

None came.

Grandpa Bucky's voice now dropped to almost a whisper. "An Indian medicine man, Apache, I believe in Arizona, blest them in a ceremony and gave them to Hoppy so he could give them to someone special if he wanted." His eye brows slowly went down until they were almost resting on the tops of his eyes.

"And, he gave them to you," said Hanky.

Grandpa Bucky's serious look returned. "I didn't say he gave them to me," he said. "I said I got them."

"But how, Grandpa," said E Jee, her excitement causing her to bounce around in front of her grandfather.

"That's where the magic comes in," said Grandpa Bucky. "And that's why I said to you both earlier, what happens in grandpa's den stays in grandpa's den."

Chapter 2

anky and E Jee didn't say a word as they retraced their path through the gangways and alleys from their Grandpa Bucky's house to their house. Each clutched a miniature leather cowboy boot in their left hand remembering the warning about everything staying in their grandfather's den.

It was the same old greeting they always got from their mother, Marie, when they walked in the back door and they gave the same old reply. "Grandpa's fine," they both said as if singing a duet. "He said to say, hi." They both scurried past their mother. "He also told us to wash behind our ears."

"Well, hi to your grandfather," she said.

"Threatened to use his Hopalong Cassidy spurs on our back sides if we misbehaved," added Hanky, a teasing smile plastered across his lips.

Their mother never commented, her chameleon brown eyes almost hidden behind her long black hair, the style having never changed since her teen-age days when she attended the Patricia Stevens Finishing School in downtown Chicago after her classes let out at Foreman High School. "Go wash your hands and get ready for dinner," she told them. "You can forget your ears until tonight."

The twins' father had no comment about their visit to his father's house. He never gave them the impression that he cared much about his father even though he deeply loved him. What the twins had always heard were enough stories about their father growing up and how hard Grandpa Bucky had treated him; getting him out of bed at five in the morning on a Saturday so he could help his father on a part-time carpentry job. They seldom heard the good. What they did hear, however, was that their grandfather was a stickler for hard work, the hard work turning out a quality job like the man named Angelo from Italy had taught young, Giuseppe. Their father had learned a lot from their Grandpa Bucky. He just didn't like the way he was taught. He did, however, like the feel of folding money in his pocket when he got paid. Sometimes the stories about their Grandpa Bucky were cloudy depending on their father's mood. What was crystal clear to the twins was that their Grandpa Bucky had been taught by the most unlikely of experts. Their grandfather's teacher had been his father-in-law, Angelo, who as a young boy had immigrated to America from the south of Italy bringing with him everything he owned in a single suitcase tied together with a rope. He also brought along with him knowledge of tools and woodworking that he had learned from his father.

Hanky and E Jee's father seldom directed a word to his children about their grandfather. When he did, which was seldom, his praises were glowing about Grandpa Bucky. He once said to Hanky and E Jee: "Your Grandpa might act a little strange with his fascination of an old television cowboy, but if you two kids ever work as hard as your grandpa did, you could act as strange as you wanted." He smiled. "You'd earn enough money to act however you wanted."

Hanky and E Jee had no clue to what their father was saying. To them he was delivering a lecture. Otherwise, almost everything else their father said, his words kept to a minimum, was directed to their mother. His favorite expression being, "What's cookin', good lookin'?" That was his way of expressing his love to her.

Dinner was inhaled, like always, by Hanky and E Jee, she sometimes wolfing down portions faster than her brother. Eating like ravenous vultures was especially true during the summer months when they didn't have homework and had their options of playing outside with their friends until dark, surfing the internet or texting on their iPhones. Most times technology won out because that's what most of their friends chose and that drove their father nuts, his inserting his favorite expression after he learned of his children's choice of activity for the evening. "Fat little couch potatoes," he would call them. "No wonder your grandfather keeps telling you to wash behind your ears." His head went from side to side. "You two are turning into a pair of Mister Potato Heads."

That same evening, Hanky and E Jee got a surprise just before they headed off for bed when their father said to them: "Your Grandpa called." They had just come in from playing outside; the street lights going on, their warning signal to get back home.

Hanky and E Jee gave their father a puzzled look. "We were just over there this afternoon to see him and Gram Gini," replied Hanky.

"I know you were," their father replied indifferently.

"Yeah, Daddy," said E Jee. "He showed us his collection of Hopalong Cassidy stuff." She grinned at her brother. "He even told us a story about how he…."

Her brother cut her off in mid-sentence with a look that told her she almost violated a trust that their Grandpa Bucky had placed in them. "He told us about how long it took him to collect all of those souvenirs he has in his den."

"My father's still calling that cave of his up in the attic his den, is he?" their father said, his comment followed by a grunt and a brief head shake. "You kids must've made a great impression on him because he wants to take you on a vacation." Their father paused and then added: "Heck, he wants to take along your mother and I plus your grandmother as well. He told me that we'd have the time of our lives."

"Vacation," echoed E Jee. "Where are we going?"

"Yeah, Dad," chimed in Hanky. "Did Grandpa say where?" Hanky caught his breath and asked hopefully, "Did he mention Disney World?"

Their father let out a loud laugh. "Disney World?" he said at the end of the laugh that had him leaning forward in his chair and grinning. "Your Grandpa would never spend money like that to go to someplace like Disney World. I think my father still has his First Communion money that he got when he was in the fourth grade. That man is so tight that he squeezes a nickel until the Indian chief belches."

Chapter 3

At first, Hanky was bummed out when he heard that his Grandpa Bucky was not taking them to Disney World or any other attraction advertising giant Ferris wheels, leaping killer whales, winding water slides or jungle safaris. "Heck," he said to his sister, we could've gone to someplace close like Six Flags. Instead, we're going to Ohio. Where in the heck is Ohio?"

Grandpa Bucky was taking his two grandchildren and their parents to the Hopalong Cassidy Museum in Cambridge, Ohio. "Hopalong Cassidy has a museum?" Hanky asked sarcastically. "Is he buried with a bunch of dead cowboys or is he wrapped up like one of those Egyptian mummies?"

"Be respectful, young man," his mother said. She had been standing nearby listening to her son throw a minor tirade. "Your grandfather is only thinking of you two kids. He thinks you two would enjoy going to Ohio to see that cowboy's museum. You both spend so much time at his house pestering him to see his collections and now you're complaining when he offers to take you to see the real thing." Inside, their mother was not thrilled about accompanying her father-in-law in his old, beat up van along with the rest of the family across Indiana to Ohio. She dreaded the trip the moment the offer had been extended. That offer, however, did not come in the form of a suggestion stating:

"How would all of you like to go on a weekend vacation to Ohio to see the Hopalong Cassidy Museum? I think the kids would really like it." That would have been the proper thing to do according to the manners and appropriate behaviors the twin's mother had been exposed to growing up; one of the key chapters in her book on etiquette.

Grandpa Bucky had been exposed to the same lessons in manners, etiquette and appropriate behavior when he was growing up. He just couldn't be bothered with being polite and appropriate, not when he was paying for it.

As time for the trip to Ohio and the Hopalong Cassidy museum got closer, Hanky's feelings began to change. He found himself getting excited and looking forward to the trip. So did E Jee. She had said to her brother, "Don't you laugh at me, Creep, but I kind of want to go to that museum to see all that Hopalong Cassidy stuff."

Hanky nodded, his eyes downcast, "Me too," he replied in a whisper so that no one would hear him. "Do you think we'll see anything magical in that museum?"

E Jee gave a shrug. "I don't know," she said. "I never thought about magical. Now all I can think about is that tiny cowboy boot in my pocket. The darned thing sometimes feels like its kicking me."

"Me too," said Hanky removing the boot from his pocket and twisting it between his thumb and forefinger the way he watched his grandfather do. He shrugged and stuffed the boot back in the right front pocket of his jeans. "I'm just curious as to how much more stuff that museum has than Grandpa."

"Jeepers creepers," said E Jee, "he sure has a lot."

Hanky grinned. "How much more stuff can there be?"

They would both find out, that and more.

Chapter 4

The trip across Indiana was sweltering and boring with both the twin's parents and their grandmother fanning themselves with sections of a Sunday Chicago Tribune that had been left scattered across the back seat of their grandfather's van for several weeks. Grandpa Bucky was not a stickler for a clean car or one that had accessories like a working air conditioner. "Always change the oil in these things," he would say to his son. "And the filters," he would quickly add. "If you don't, you're asking for trouble." There would be a grunt or two from him before he continued sounding like an auto mechanic instead of a retired fireman. "Brakes, tires and plugs," he would add to his check-off list of car maintenance items. "If the guts on these cars are in working order, you'll never have a problem and won't be shelling out all kinds of dough to some greedy mechanic who will overcharge you."

Comfort was not on Grandpa Bucky's maintenance list for his van. Neither was cleanliness, and that included inside and out. His van appeared not to have been washed since before Henry John and Elsa Jane were born. If wrappers from fast food restaurants had coded dates on them, his might have had a wrapper from the first McDonald's in Des Plaines, Illinois back in the 1950's stuffed under the driver's front seat.

The warm humid air progressed to hot and stifling where

breathing became more like chewing the air as the day dragged on and the van sped east toward its destination. "Couple three more hours and we'll be there said Grandpa Bucky without looking over his shoulder. "Anybody hungry or have to go potty?" he asked softly, hoping no one would hear him. All of his passengers heard his question and he was forced to pull off the Indiana Toll Road at the last plaza where he got gas and the others went to the restrooms. He found himself reluctantly treating his passengers to hamburgers, fries and large soft drinks brimming with ice; both his wife and daughter-in-law getting spare cups of ice.

"Do you know what they have inside that plaza, Dad?" Grandpa Bucky's daughter-in-law asked as she handed him a large cup filled with ice water. She didn't wait for his answer. "It's called air conditioning!" she shouted, uncharacteristically of her. "People inside look cool, comfortable and relaxed," she continued, her volume not declining. "They don't look like they've been stewing in their own juices for hours riding in a four wheel sauna."

"Thanks for the ice water, Daughter-in-Law and my son's lovely beauty queen and Miss Northwest Side Springtime of nineteen hundred whenever," he said. He took a sip of his ice water, smiled and added another, "Thanks."

"You got the stewing in our own juices right, Marie," said Gini, her commented directed into her husband's ear. "I just hope we all don't pass out before we get to the air conditioned motel you reserved for us. It does have air conditioning, doesn't it?"

Grandpa Bucky nodded, didn't say a word and took another sip of his ice water. He gave a second nod, turned the ignition key and smiled at the loud, rumbling sound the van's rusted out muffler made. "The Hopalong Cassidy Express is now departing on track number nine," he said over his shoulder to his passengers in the back of the van. "All aboard."

Five sullen and perspiring people reluctantly clicked on their seat belts.

They had crossed over the Indiana state line into the Buckeye State with no one noticing. Before long the van was approaching Cambridge, Ohio and Grandpa Bucky turned very serious. He sensed his passengers' discomfort was increasing by the minute. That was made evident by the increased acceleration of their makeshift paper fans that were now showing signs of starting to disintegrate making the fan appear to have been hit by snow flurries.

Grandpa Bucky's serious mode got even more serious. Once in town, he kept glancing at a piece of paper he had sitting on his lap. He didn't say a word. After a while, he made a right turn after waiting for the person in front of him to get off what looked like a cell phone. "Village idiot," he muttered at the unidentifiable motorist. "You tryin' to kill me or somethin'?" Grandpa Bucky then made a left turn onto a busy street. He saw it immediately. The motel where he made reservations for his family was less than a block ahead. A smile crossed his face as he pulled into the motel's parking lot, the sign flashing, *No Vacancy*. He ignored comments from his wife, son and daughter-in-law knowing better than to pour gas on their combined simmering fires and gave a glance to the back seat of the van where Hanky and E Jee were sitting as if to say, "I don't want to hear it from you two either."

The others in the car continued to pummel the sultry, humid air with their ink smeared paper fans as they watched Grandpa Bucky, their chauffeur and tour guide, get out of the van and enter the motel. He was only in the office several minutes when he emerged with a man about his age that was much taller than their grandfather, skinnier and bald. They were both laughing like two old friends who hadn't seen one another in years. They were old friends and they hadn't seen each other in years.

Hanky and E Jee were introduced by their grandfather to a tall, jovial balding man named, Mushy who quickly invited them into motel's office. "Just like this guy to keep you all out in this heat and humidity," said Mushy, while giving several nods to Grandpa Bucky who stood alongside of him. Mushy had a continuous sucking chuckle that sounded like a semi-truck tire leaking air. "Always thinking of himself and that gosh danged Hopalong Cassidy," he continued on as he glanced in the back seat of the van just as Hanky and E Jee were getting out. "Did your grandpa ever tell you about the time at the circus when he booed Hopalong Cassidy?"

"Whoa," shouted Grandpa Bucky. "You know darn good and well I would never boo Hoppy.

Hanky and E Jee couldn't believe that their grandfather had gotten them their own motel room. Their parents had their own room and their grandparents had their own, the biggest room in the motel that was a kitchenette. None of them cared. There was air conditioning and each room was comfortable and clean if not a bit on the worn side.

Hanky remembered instantly that Grandpa Bucky's friend, Mushy was one of boys mentioned when their grandfather had told him the story about being interrogated by a nun as to who had booed Hopalong Cassidy at the circus. Mushy wasn't even an altar boy, but he, according to their grandfather, got the third degree from Sister Mary Helen. Hanky and E Jee weren't interested in old stories from when their grandfather was their age. They had their own room and a television that was hooked to cable and had more stations than their flat screen television's at home with the basic cable package. They had also heard their father say way too often, "Why should I pay the national debt each month so I can have five hundred stations filled with donkey dung?"

That night, Mushy and his wife, Penelope, had the Goodson family for dinner in their apartment located behind the motel's office. Penelope was of Greek heritage. She had shoulder length black hair that seemed to be illuminated by a spotlight and rich olive colored skin that brought an obvious look of envy from both Gram Gini and Marie. That night the envy grew as the Goodson family enjoyed a feast of Penelope's country's special foods. Hanky and E Jee didn't know what to make of stuffed vine leaves, something that resembled lasagna and cheese that was served on fire. They ate the Moussaka after they were told it was the Greek version of macaroni and cheese. Mushy's wife also made a pork roast with homemade dumplings and red cabbage to satisfy her husband's Czech ancestral taste buds; it was also a treat for Grandpa Bucky who had spent many a Sunday afternoon at the Mushy's house when they were growing up and playing together; his play time coinciding with the noon meal on Sunday.

After the long, tiring, hot drive, Hanky, E Jee and their parents were in their rooms sleeping soundly while Grandpa and Grandma Goodson stayed visiting with their hosts. Sleep came fast and Hanky couldn't wait for the morning to get there so they could get to the Hopalong Cassidy Museum. Had he known what awaited him and his sister, he wouldn't have been so anxious and, perhaps, not as cocky as his grandfather once had been on the day Hopalong Cassidy was booed.

Chapter 5

"Geez, will you look at all this stuff," Hanky said to E Jee as they stood in the largest of the open rooms that made up the museum feeling overwhelmed by the sheer amount of memorabilia displayed on the walls and shelves of the old building. The museum was definitely a Nirvana for Hopalong Cassidy enthusiasts. "Grandpa doesn't have a fraction of these Hoppy things that are in here."

E Jee nodded at her brother. "Hopalong Cassidy must've been one famous dude back in the old days, Hanky." Her head didn't move, but her eyes went from side to side, a look of awe replacing her usual string of excited words. She found herself unable to talk as she looked at the displays, seeing everything, but seeing nothing, drinking in sight after sight, absorbing scene after scene. So many old movie posters were overwhelming, confusing her, taking away her ability to focus, clouding her choices so she didn't know what to look at next. She found herself silently counting, not believing that one ancient Hollywood cowboy could have made so many movies. Her counting was interrupted when she had reached sixty and felt a tug on her arm. She almost jumped out of her skin. "You, Jerk-o," she said annoyed. "You made me lose my count." She sighed and said to her brother, "I bet Grandpa Bucky doesn't know that Hopalong Cassidy made so many movies. Before you had to butt in, I counted at least sixty posters on the wall. Gee, Hanky, over sixty. Can you believe it?" She glanced at her brother who was indicating that she should follow him.

"Look," he said quietly to his sister as he pointed with his left hand across the room in the opposite direction from where they were standing. He cast a glance in the direction of the others who hadn't noticed what had grabbed his attention.

E Jee looked at where her brother's finger was pointing. "What am I supposed to be looking at, Hanky?"

"There," he said, his finger making thrusting actions in the direction of a short wall that was void of Hopalong Cassidy relics.

"That door with the rope in front of it?" she asked.

"Is there any other door over there," said Hanky losing patience.

Something else had also grabbed both of their attentions. They didn't realize it at first. Then it hit them. It was the feel of a tiny leather cowboy boot each carried in their right front pocket. Each boot had started to give a gentle kick, a warning sign. The twins didn't notice the warning.

Hanky, with E Jee alongside of him, stood by a door that had what looked like a thick rope in front of it to block the entrance. The rope looked like velvet and was a faded, dusty black in color and hooked up to two brass stanchions badly in need of a polishing. There was a cardboard sign hanging from the center of the rope that sported one word that looked like it had been printed in crayon. The sign read: *Private.*

The sign only increased Hanky's curiosity. He took a quick glance over his shoulder and saw that the adults were talking to a lady that had introduced herself as a tour guide. "Come on," he said, grabbing his sister by the hand as he squatted down and crawled under the black rope.

"But, it says private," E Jee protested without digging in her heels.

Hanky gave another tug on his sister's arm. "Yeah, but it don't say nothing about keeping out. What does private mean anyway?"

"I think it means to keep out," said E Jee, her explanation hushed. "You know exactly what it means. We haven't been in Ohio for a full day and already you're trying to get us in trouble." She tried to free her arm from her brother's grip. "Gee willickers, Hanky I just know nothing good is going to come of this."

Another tug on E Jee's arm and Hanky was reaching out with his other hand for the door knob. "Don't worry, Sis," Hanky said trying to sound brave, even bold. "If someone catches us, we'll just play dumb. We'll act like a couple of stupid kids who accidentally ended up in a place they shouldn't have been in. What kind of trouble can we get into?"

They both found out as they entered a room that was a fraction of the size of their room at the motel. The two of them froze when they saw a man dressed in a black western style shirt and matching black pants seated on a rickety looking cane back chair at a small dressing table. He was smoking a cigarette and he wore a pair of white sweat socks, a small hole at each big toe. His feet were propped up on the table and he appeared to be engrossed in how far each big toe could be poked through the hole. He turned and looked at Hanky and E Jee as if their entering the room was an everyday occurrence. "Two more dummies who can't read," he muttered nodding at the door. "The sign says, 'private'," he said in a calm voice. "What part of the word don't you two understand? The private or the private as in private keep out."

Hanky and E Jee both blushed as they watched the man who had silver wavy hair take a drag on his cigarette then letting the smoke slowly escape from his mouth, the smell causing E Jee's eyes to water.

"We're sorry," Hanky said sounding sincere. "We thought the sign meant there was a private collection of more Hoppy stuff in here." He paused hoping the man was buying his story and that they wouldn't get into trouble.

The man took another puff on his cigarette, flicked an ash into a waste basket by the side of the dressing table. The waste basket had a picture of Hopalong Cassidy on it. "Stuff," he said sounding amused. "That collection out in the museum of thirty years isn't enough stuff, as you call it," he said, his words now sounding both sarcastic and annoyed. That collection out there isn't big enough for you two so you came in here looking for more," he said as he removed his feet from the top of the dressing table. "How come you two are such William Boyd aficionados?" the man asked, his face still showing amusement, but not his eyes. "Or, don't you know the meaning of aficionado?"

"Our Grandpa Bucky is the Hoppy fan," said Hanky.

"Jeepers creepers," echoed E Jee her voice showing excitement as her words fired out. "Our grandpa has a whole wall of shelves full of Hopalong Cassidy stuff in his den at home."

"Now does he?" the man replied to E Jee. He stood up and didn't appear much taller than either their dad or their grandfather. The man's amusement never changed but his eyes seemed to turn darker becoming almost a sinister black in color.

He let out a gruff laugh. "So, you two want to see more Hoppy stuff as you call it," he said, the amusement suddenly gone from him.

Hanky and E Jee saw the change in the man instantly. "Yes, Sir," replied Hanky. "We just thought there might be some extra special private stuff in here. That's why we looked."

"Is that so," said the man as he reached out and his left hand grabbed Hanky by the shoulder and his right hand latched onto E Jee's shoulder.

"Grandpa was right," thought E Jee. "I didn't expect that man to grab my shoulder."

The man's hands clamped down on the twins' shoulders giving them a squeeze for a moment before giving Hanky and E Jee a gentle push in the direction opposite the door they had entered. They were headed toward a black velvet curtain that hung across what appeared to be a door opening. "If it's more stuff you want to see, then it's more stuff you two are going to get."

"We didn't mean no harm," said Hanky, knowing he should be making a dash for the private door they had entered earlier. He couldn't move. Neither could E Jee.

The miniature boots in the twins' pockets were kicking like crazy. If those boots could have spoken, they would have both shouted out warnings to the twins to turn and run as fast as they could.

No words came from the boots only the feeling that they were trying to jump out of their respective pockets. The boots felt as if they had spurs attached and the spurs were piercing in the side of each twin's thigh. Both reached down on the outside of their jeans and grabbed at the shape of the boot that had seemed to grow. They squeezed hoping to somehow crush the tiny boots and put an end to the growing pain. Before either of the twins could squeeze any harder, they both felt themselves being given a hard shove and propelled through the black curtain. The shove, however, was not a shove. It was more like someone had tied each of them to a medieval catapult and cut them loose. They weren't being pushed through the black curtain. They were being propelled, lifted off the floor and hurled forward. There was no feel of the man's hands on them. There was no man in black period. Both Hanky and E Jee were being jettisoned through the black opening by an invisible force that felt like a giant magnet had a grip on them, pulling them through space. In an instant they were being struck in the face by a fierce wind, their hands and arms pinned to their sides. Fighting was useless. Then nervous changed to fear when several flashes of lightning and deafening blasts of thunder engulfed them. Next they heard a loud, thundering rumble that sounded like the museum was crumbling to the ground. Instinctively, both of them smashed the palms of their hands against their ears. The noise only grew louder. They both stared, void of feeling, trying to see. They couldn't see. Hanky reached for his sister's hand, but all he got was the reach. There was nothing. "E Jee!" he screamed. Her name came out as a long, chilling echo. He started to call her name again and then felt himself starting to spin as if he had been turned into a giant child's toy. That was the last thing he remembered.

When Hanky opened his eyes he found himself looking into

the eyes of his twin sister. They were both lying on their sides facing each other. Their eyes made recognition, but they couldn't talk. Slowly, as if on cue, they both made a cautious roll away from each other. It was only a half a roll, but it was enough to make them gasp. They couldn't believe what they saw.

E Jee grabbed on to Hanky's arm almost tearing it off from his shoulder. "Where are we?" she asked, sounding in a state of panic, her other hand taking hold in a vice like grip.

Hanky turned looking for the black curtain, but it was gone. He blinked, and then blinked again not liking or understanding what he saw. He tried not to tremble and scare his sister, but he lost, and so did E Jee.

"I don't believe it," said Hanky.

"Where are we?" E Jee asked again, both her fear and shaking unwilling to ease up. "Where's that silver haired man in the holey sweat socks?' she asked cautiously.

"I dunno," said Hanky. "The creep pushed us through that door."

E Jee spun around as if she were a needle on a compass and looked at her brother. "Where's the door, Hanky? I don't see any door."

Hanky did a slow turn, his eyes searching. He didn't see anything that resembled a room, or black velvet, a door or a museum. "We're on some kind of ranch," he said. Then quickly adding, "It looks like something from an old western movie; like some of those old black and white ones we watched on that DVD set that Grandpa Bucky gave us." They both were scared out of their wits and shook like scrawny saplings in a windstorm.

"You said the magic word, Hanky," said E Jee. "Home; and that's where I want to be." She grabbed her brother by the hand.

"Come on. Let's see if we can find that black velvet curtain that we got pushed through by that old, grey haired man smoking that stinky cigarette."

Hanky's head went back and forth and then he turned completely around. "E Jee, I don't see no black velvet curtain. I don't see no door," he said, his head still twisting, his eyes searching. "And, I don't see no grey haired man with his toes sticking through his socks either." He caught his breath. "All I see are a bunch of cows mooing and pooping behind that big fence in front of us." He paused and looked some more. "Is that barbed wire?" he asked. "That's got to be a corral. And the biggest one I've ever seen. I ain't never seen so many cows either."

E Jee suddenly shed her fear and punched her brother in his upper arm. "That's the only corral you've ever seen except in the movies, you dufus. And the only cows you've ever seen are the ones in the fields along the roads when Grandpa Bucky took us and Daddy fishing to one of his special places way up in Wisconsin."

Hanky rubbed at his arm and said, "Whad ya hit me for?"

"Because you can act so stupid at times," she said as she grabbed her brother by the hand and started pulling him along. "And, we're not looking at cows either. Geez, don't you remember a thing from those old cowboy movies we've seen?"

Hanky nodded defiantly then muttered, "Hey, who died and made you Queen of the Corral?"

"No one," she shot back. "But I do know those are cattle and not cows." She continued to pull her brother along.

Hanky suddenly stopped and yanked his hand free. "Where you pullin' me, Miss Girl Scout of the Year?" he asked.

His sister gave a nod in the direction at the opposite end of the large corral where a single story, dark grey frame house stood. The house had a front porch with a roof overhang and was about four football fields in length from where they were standing.

E Jee pulled her brother in earnest in that direction. They could both see that what appeared to be smoke coming from a stone chimney rising up from the left side of the house. At the same time, they each felt tiny cowboy boots prodding them to head in the direction of the house.

"Do you think we should go there?" asked Hanky pulling back on his sister's hand. "I've already got us in enough trouble for dragging us into a place we shouldn't have been in." He dug in harder.   "Are you trying to get us into deeper trouble by trespassing into someone's house?"

"Maybe there's someone in there who can help us," said E Jee. She yanked back on her brother's hand as hard as she could. "Come on, Hanky," she said determined but sounding as if she were pleading. "It can't hurt."

"And, maybe it can," replied Hanky with reluctance. "I ain't so sure about that." He continued to look around. "Did you ever bother to ask yourself why you're standing out here in the middle of a desert and how exactly you got here?" He didn't give his sister a chance to answer. "Look around," he said pointing at the mountains looming up all around them in the distance. "We ain't got no mountains like that in Chicago," he continued. "And, I sure didn't see any mountains in Ohio or around Hoppy's museum. Did you?"

E Jee simply gave a shrug.

Hanky turned to his left and pointed. "If I'm not mistaken, those aren't ant hills we're lookin' at," he said being sarcastic. He turned a bit more and continued to point. "Looks like we just might also be stuck in the biggest sand pile that I've ever seen," he continued. "And, those things with the goofy looking green arms are some kind of cactus plants. Didn't we see one of those in an old John Wayne cowboy movie where he took out a big knife and hacked open one of those things and found water for he and his men to drink?"

Just then they heard what sounded like a faint thunder coming from behind them. They both turned and could see what looked like wisps of clouds far off in the distance coming from the base of the mountains.

"Come on, Hanky, run," said E Jee pulling on her brother's hand in earnest. "I don't like the feeling I'm getting about all of this. Grandpa Bucky's magic boot is kicking the bee jeepers out of me."

Hanky followed E Jee who was now into a full sprint heading for the house. She closed the distance from the corral fence in a matter of seconds. "Don't look back!" shouted E Jee. "It'll slow you down."

The thunder grew louder and the faint clouds took on a dark, sinister shape. What scared them both was that they could also make out faint, black shapes that appeared to be people riding horses, and riding the horses fast. What added to their fear was there looked like a small group of several people on horseback out in front of the larger group. "Gosh," said E Jee, "those people look like they're being chased." Then they both heard a loud noise and raced to the house where they took the front porch steps three at a time. They heard the same noise again as they stopped and turned on the wooden landing of the porch.

"Did you hear that?" asked E Jee, her eyes growing wider. "Is someone back there shooting a gun, Hanky?"

"I heard it," said Hanky. He paused. "That sure sounded like gunshots to me."

"You think?" asked E Jee now clinging to her brother's arm.

They both jumped. There was the sound of more gunshots. Then there was the sound of a door opening and a woman's voice asking, "What are you two young 'uns doing here?"

Before they could answer there were several more gunshots, and the riders being chased became more distinct as did those doing the chasing.

"Inside, you two," said the woman in a tough voice that started them both. She was about the age of Hanky and E Jee's mother and wore jeans, cowboy boots, a bright red blouse that was adorned with white fringes on the sleeves and breast pockets. There was something else that both Hanky and E Jee couldn't believe. The lady was wearing a gun belt with twin holsters; two white pearl handled six guns stood looking like they were ready to be put into action. Two things that Hanky and E Jee could agree on were that they were scared stiff and that the miniature cowboy boots that their grandfather had given them were trying to jump out of their pockets.

"Geez," those are just like the Hopalong Cassidy cap pistol set that Grandpa Bucky has," said Hanky his head nodding at the pistols the woman wore.

"I don't think those are cap pistols," replied E Jee as she followed the woman into the house.

As the door slammed shut, the woman took a quick look out of the window that was smeared with dust and dirt and covered by faded white lace curtains. "Get under that kitchen table," she ordered. "And be quiet."

The twins followed the woman's orders but not before noticing both of her hands going to the grips of the white pearl handled pistols.

Chapter 6

Hanky and E Jee had gone to their knees and scooted under the heavy wooden table made of dark grey, streaked weathered boards that looked like they had been beaten with a hammer. A small, white lace doily sat in the middle of the table with a clear glass vase holding a single yellow flower. Both Hanky and E Jee had their backs up against the wall and their knees pulled tightly to their chests held in death grip hugs by their arms and hands. Their eyes did all the talking for them as they obeyed the lady with the two six guns. Neither said a word.

"Gosh darn, Ringo," muttered the lady, her eyes shifting between her young visitors curled up in twin balls under the table and then to the dirty window next to the front door. She counted five riders racing under the arched entrance to her ranch. "Well, I'll be," she said, sounding relieved as she recognized the five riders. "That guy always shows up when a person needs a helpin' hand." She reached for the door handle. "Maybe now I can pay him back for what he's done for me over these years.

Hanky could make out that the lady's free hand was still gripping the handle of one of her six guns, but she didn't remove it from the holster.

E Jee's eyes were also riveted on the women's hands gripping the pistols' shiny handles, but for a different reason. These hands were entirely different than her mothers. Her mom was always filing her nails, especially while watching television. After, there would be nail polish applied; often multiple coats depending on whether a critical inspection for any flaws could be passed. The number of nail polish coats always won out over the number of inspections. This woman's nails were not those of E Jee's mother and her hands looked as if they had been used to dig post holes for barbed wire fencing. E Jee didn't see enough nails at the end of the gnarly, calloused fingers that had space for polish. "Gosh," thought E Jee, as her eyes settled on the woman's plain face void of all make-up and surrounded by blond hair, "that lady sure is pretty."

The twins saw the woman's hand give the door handle a quick turn about the time they heard the clatter of boots coming up the stairs. Hanky saw the door burst open and five sets of scuffed, dust covered boots, all with spurs, stomped into the room. Then the door slammed shut with a bang.

"Thanks, Miss Jab," one of the men said in a voice that Hanky thought sounded familiar. "Ringo and that band of cut throats sure want your cattle in the worst way."

"They can want 'til Hades freezes over," said the woman who now had a name. "But, gosh darn it they ain't gettin' one head of my cattle." She paused. "And they'd better get off of this here ranch if they know what's good for them."

Easy, Miss Jab," said the man with the familiar voice. "Me and the boys will get rid of that nasty bunch for you. No need for you to get worked up and in a dither over some folks that don't know right from wrong."

"Mister Cassidy, you may have changed my life and made me a law abiding, God fearin' woman, but none of that made me forget how to handle these," she said, drawing her guns from their holsters.

Hanky and E Jee's pushed their backs so hard against the wall they thought they heard the boards crack and feared that they might end up outside on the front porch. They were bending slightly forward trying to get a glimpse of who belonged to the five sets of boots and spurs. "Did you hear what she called that guy?" Hanky asked his sister. "She said, Mister Cassidy. Do ya think?"

E Jee gave a shrug.

"And you won't be needing those fancy, lady like shootin' irons you got your hands wrapped around," said the man. "You don't need to do no more jail time for shootin' someone; no matter how mean and nasty a varmint he might be."

"I know that, Mister Cassidy," said the lady that had been addressed as Miss Jab. "If it weren't for you getting me out of that awful prison in the middle of nowhere because of that trumped up charge of cattle rustling, I'd still be behind bars. You've been more than a big help to me and my goin' straight and tryin' to run this here ranch. I don't forget good folks, Mister Cassidy and you and your boys, well, y'all good folks."

One word had Hanky and E Jee staring at one another as if they had come face-to-face with the Devil. "She did say, Cassidy," said Hanky. "I knew I heard it right the first time."

E Jee replied with a nervous nod. "But she didn't say a thing about him being called Hopalong." Her index finger went quickly to her lips when she noticed her brother was going to say something else.

Hanky nodded.

"That sure is the Ringo bunch," another male voice said. This one old sounding and raspy making the speaker sound as if his throat were lined with the sand and rocky soil outside.

"You got that right, Chats," replied another voice, this one young sounding. "That bunch has the Ringo brand stamped all over them." There was a pause. "Who ever heard of a cattle brand in the shape of a skull and cross bones? Gosh darnedest thing I ever did see."

"Ringo's desperadoes, little brother, that's who," answered a voice that sounded exactly like the one that had asked the pirate question.

"How 'bout it, Hoppy," said another voice, this one masculine and serious. "The five of us can mow down those scum in nothin' flat. Just give the word."

"It is Hoppy," said Hanky, his words flying out of his mouth in a gasp. He fought the urge to scoot out from under the wooden table and introduce himself to Hopalong Cassidy. Before he could say another word, he was looking into the smiling face of a white haired man wearing a black hat. He had sparkling friendly eyes that looked like a spotlight was shining on them and they seem to be asking why a young boy and a girl were under the table.

"I don't know who they are or where they came from, Mister Cassidy," said Miss Jab. "All I saw was that Ringo bunch chasing after you and your boys and, the next thing I know, well, I've got these two young 'uns as house guests."

Hanky and E Jee saw a hand appear under the table and motion for them to come out. They gave each other a relieved look and scooted out from under the table on the seat of their pants. Both brushed off the seat of their jeans and then quickly went to their knees before standing in front of the lady known as

Miss Jab. They immediately saw the others in the room. One of the men was no older looking than their father; two looked like brothers who were teenagers and there was an older man with deep rugged crevices around his eyes. He looked as old as their Grandpa Bucky. He had shaggy grey hair and an equally shaggy beard. The fifth man captivated their attention. They knew they were looking up at Hopalong Cassidy.

"Gee willickers," said a surprised E Jee. "You're Hopalong Cassidy."

"That's my name, Missy," said Hoppy, his eyes still sparkling and flashing a warm welcome. "And you are?"

"I'm E Jee," she shot back. "My real name is Elsa Jane Goodson. My Confirmation name is Gertrude, but my mother only calls me that when she's mad at me and that doesn't happen very often because, most times, I'm good, Mister Cassidy. I really am. Geez, I really mean it.'

"I'm sure you are and I'm sure you do, Missy," replied Hopalong Cassidy his smile growing with each of E Jee's words.

Hanky took a bold step toward Hopalong Cassidy and put out his hand. "I'm E Jee's older brother, Hoppy, and it sure is a pleasure to meet you. I've been a fan of yours all my life."

"That long," said the old man named Chats. "Must be goin' on twelve to thirteen years it looks to me."

"Mind your manners, Chats," said Hoppy. "This polite young fella is introducing himself and polite is a commodity I don't see too much of coming from you boys." He paused and looked at the two younger members of his group. "Of course, Tim and Tom are more than polite when they're around those dance hall girls in town." He paused and look at the two young cowboys. "At least they're polite for awhile. Then some cowpokes try to take the girls their dancing with away from them."

It was Chats who interrupted. "Those two over there, Tim/Tom or Tom/Tim are also known as T 'n T, because of their explosive personalities." He let out a laugh that resembled a cackle. "More than one unlucky cowboy has found that out."

Tim and Tom blushed while the others, except Hanky and E Jee, roared with laughter. They were too much in awe to do anything but be respectful to the others in the room. Respectful, as they had been taught by their parents, especially their father was what children did in the presence of adults. He had instructed them in his own unique way to mind their business. As he put it, "Be sure your brain is engaged before your tongue moves. In other words, keep your big mouths shut unless you are spoken to."

"Our Grandpa Bucky's a huge fan of yours like we are," said E Jee, her courage coming out while her comfort level continued to soar. She wasn't about to be outdone by her brother. "Mister Cassidy," she started out wide-eyed. "My brother is only a couple of minutes older than me. We're twins," she continued. "But we're both big fans. Our Grandpa Bucky is the biggest fan."

"Now what's this word, fan, I've heard mention twice now mean?" Hopalong Cassidy asked being even more polite than Hanky and E Jee.

Hanky and E Jee started to explain, both talking at the same time, their excited words leaping out.

Hopalong Cassidy put up both hands a chuckle making its way out of his smiling lips. "Whoa," he said. "Not so fast." He glanced at E Jee. "Where I come from pretty ladies always go first before men folk."

E Jee made a face at her brother and started. Her words were spilling out so fast it appeared that she wasn't breathing. By the time she had finished covering Grandpa Bucky's den, his Hoppy collection, the ride to Ohio, meeting Mister Mushy and his wife, Penelope and Hoppy being booed at the circus, Hoppy stood with arms folded across his chest looking both puzzled and amused.

"I did all of that?" he asked.

"And more," added Hanky, finding his opportunity to jump into the conversation.

Hoppy pursed his lips and pushed his black hat back slightly showing more of his white hair. "Why would someone what to boo me?" he asked. "There are men out there who want to shoot me and others who have; one in particular. That's how I got my name." He paused and looked at both Hanky and E Jee. "But I don't remember anyone ever booing me." He paused for a moment, thinking. "Then again," he began to say before cutting himself off.

Just then a shot hit the front door of the ranch house, the board where the bullet hit splintering before it continued on, stopping as it buried itself in the back wall. Before they realized what had happened, Hoppy had pushed Hanky and E Jee under the table saying, "Back you go." He had his guns drawn. All the others had their six shooters drawn except Chats who was carrying a Winchester lever action 30-30. Hoppy quickly signaled with both of his guns, one waving to the right and the other to the left. Chats quickly moved into position by the left window facing the corral. Miss Jab, her guns drawn and the hammers cocked, stayed next to Hoppy while the youngest cowboys, Tim and Tom moved to the right of the window. The other cowboy in Hoppy's group, the man who appeared to be as old as their father, but slightly younger than Hoppy, had taken a position at the other window. He had been addressed as Randy and he only spoke when he was spoken to.

Hanky and E Jee sat on the floor with their knees pulled up to their chins again; this time even harder. They had heard and seen a bullet splinter part of a wooden door and realized it wasn't the same as a cloud of dust out in the desert caused by galloping horses. Their faces showed fear as they forced their heads down and tried to ram their backs up against the wall even harder than before.

"Stay cool, Sis," whispered Hanky. "Nothin' is gonna happen to us with Hoppy here. You're gonna be safe. Understand?"

E Jee never showed her face as her head barely went up and down. "If the way that magic boot in my pocket is kicking, we're going to be either safe or sorry."

"What's your business, Ringo?" Hoppy shouted from the side of the door that was splintered. He was careful to stand against the wall for protection from any other shots that might be fired.

"Some of those cattle in the corral belong to us and we aim to take what's rightfully ours," hollered Ringo.

"Whatever's rightfully yours and sports your Jolly Roger brand should belong to you," Hoppy hollered back. "But, you ain't takin' what don't belong to you. At last count, every steer in that corral belongs to Miss Jab; the sheriff said so."

"I don't care what no sheriff said," hollered back Ringo. "We aim to take what's ours and you and no sheriff and all the lawmen in this here Arizona territory ain't gonna stop us."

There was silence as Hoppy looked at Miss Jab and gave her knowing nod. Another nod went to his men, this one indicating that he was going to open the door and face the head of the group of cattle rustlers. "Cover me," he said to his men as he reached for the door handle.

Hanky and E Jee quickly saw their fear joined by the urge to get up and run. They didn't. Hanky reached over and put his arm around E Jee who was fighting tears. They heard the door open and Hoppy called out to Ringo: "I'm comin' out so we can talk this out." Hanky saw Hoppy put a hand through the open door. "See, Ringo, no gun." He moved partially out the door and showed his other hand. "You wouldn't shoot an unarmed man now would you, Ringo?" Then Hoppy was outside standing on the porch.

There was silence inside the ranch house except for the cocking of the pistols and Chats pushing and pulling on the Winchester's lever injecting a bullet into the rifle's well oiled chamber. Chats may have appeared to look unclean, but he kept his trusty Winchester spotless and well oiled, the wooden stock coated with linseed oil whenever he got the rare chance to carefully rub it into the wood that glistened like the day Chats bought it in a Wichita, Kansas general store when he was the age of Tim and Tom.

Hanky squeezed his sister's shoulder, closed his eyes and held his breath.

Chapter 7

anky and E Jee could feel the tension building in the room as Hoppy and Ringo confronted one another. They were shouting, Ringo more than Hoppy, so they could be heard over the noise of the cattle that were becoming more agitated. All the parties knew it wouldn't take much to scare the herd and have them bust through the corral fence gate and stampede out of control thundering in a helter-skelter direction known only to them.

All of the weapons in the room were being pointed at predetermined targets if anyone from the other side started shooting. For sure, Ringo would lose at least five, perhaps six or seven of his gang before they could fire off a second round of shots. Everyone in the room was concerned for Hoppy's safety.

Hoppy seemed at ease on the front porch of the ranch house. He had intentionally positioned himself by the right hand railing of the front porch by design. If the shooting did start, he would vault over the railing and dive for cover under the porch. The porch steps would take away the line of fire angle Ringo and his men had on him and Hoppy knew that Ringo was a bad shot; most of his victims having been shot in the back. He was known all over the Arizona territory and even north into Kansas and Missouri for only being able to hit a target if he was standing behind it and close. What Ringo and his men didn't know is that

Hoppy had both his guns tucked firmly into his holster belt in the back of his pants. Empty holsters appeared to be just that— empty. But Hoppy knew from experience that men like Ringo were never to be trusted.

Neither Hanky nor E Jee knew this at first. The others, including Miss Jab did. Both of her white handled pistols were on her targets. Ringo was one target and his saddle partner to the right who she thought looked familiar was the other. If she noticed a trigger finger start to squeeze, that cowboy would be a candidate for Boot Hill.

"I've got a proposal for you, Ringo," Hoppy hollered to his adversary as he placed his left boot on the lower rail of the porch banister.

"What is it?" Ringo hollered back. "I'm still taking what belongs to me, and most of them cattle are mine."

"They were yours," muttered Miss Jab but not loud enough for anyone outside, including Hoppy, to hear. "I wasted two years in that prison thanks to you and your bandits for framing me in that rustling scheme. This here lady don't forget that easy and you're going to pay for what you did to me."

Hanky's arm pulled E Jee closer to him. "We'll be okay," he said trying to reassure his sister that no harm would come to them. "Hoppy will protect us. I promise." He hoped he could convince his sister that they would somehow get back to their parents and the Hopalong Cassidy museum in Ohio from wherever they were out in the desert? Then he heard Ringo holler out to Hoppy.

"Your plan better be a good one, Cassidy or you and your men might find your remains being feasted on by a hungry pack of coyotes!"

"No need for violence, Ringo," said Hoppy as if he were having a Sunday afternoon talk with a minister after church services. If you send two of your men into the corral, I'll send in two of mine. Whatever cattle you find in there with your brand on them, well, you take them. They're yours; just like you say. If your boys don't find anything, then you ride off and let Miss Jab run her ranch. She paid her dues, as unjust as they were, to society and society said she's a free woman. You wouldn't go against the law now, would you, Ringo?"

Ringo let out a gruff laugh. Then he said something to the two men on horseback sitting to each side of him that Hoppy didn't hear. Hoppy anticipated trouble and was coiled up and ready to leap for cover. Six more mounted riders were behind Ringo. Heads nodded up and down several times and then Ringo and his men holstered their weapons. "You can't spend the rest of your life on this here ranch with that cattle rustling gun slinging woman," he said. "You might think you're winning a show down now, but think again, Cassidy. Me and my boys will be back to collect our beef steak!" There was a pause as Ringo turned his horse to ride away. "And, we're going to collect all of it, Cassidy. I think you're going to need a lot more guns the next time."

"I don't think there'll be a next time, Ringo," Hoppy shouted back. Ringo and his men didn't hear him, but Hanky, E Jee, Miss Jab and the others inside did. It was Miss Jab who heard him loud and clear and she was making mental preparations for the next show down.

Hoppy stood on the porch, his boot still on the lower rail of the banister and watched the horsemen ride off. He detested violence and bloodshed of any kind, but had never backed down from a fight preferring to use his fists than his guns. He had been shot once in his life, that in the left leg giving him his name Hopalong. Over the years, his limp became barely noticeable and he developed a reputation for being a straight shooter and someone who could be called on to help those who were being picked on or bullied.

Hanky and E Jee peeked out from under the table to see Miss Jab partially open the door. "Everything okay, Hoppy?" she asked.

"The air's fresh and clear out here now," replied Hoppy, both feet now resting firmly on the porch. "Come on out and enjoy the Arizona Territory sunshine. It's looking mighty fine and feeling good."

All the others joined Hoppy on the porch as Hanky and E Jee crawled out from under the table and quickly fell in behind them. E Jee was almost in the rear pocket of Miss Jab's jeans. Hoppy gave the woman a serious look. "Miss Jab," he said his word coming out cautious. "I don't think you've seen the end of Ringo. He and his boys are up to no good and I'm sure they'll be back." He paused and gazed out over the cattle that had settled down in their confinement. "I'd be willing to bet my horse, Topper that Ringo will be recruiting more guns before the day is over." His eyes traveled to the others. "We can expect him back real soon," he said not sounding worried. "By tomorrow I'm willing to bet;

maybe before sun up."

"I know I haven't seen the last of that no good sidewinder," Miss Jab replied sounding like someone gearing up for a fight. "What am I going to do, Hoppy?" she asked. "I can't fight off that crook's army of no good vermin by myself. Even if my two kids were here to help me, we wouldn't have a chance against all those guns Ringo pays for. I never knew there were that many blood thirsty, greedy mavericks scattered across the territory."

Hoppy gave her a reassuring smile. "You know, Miss Jab there's more than one way to take care of a cheating, conniving scoundrel like Ringo."

"Oh," she replied in almost a whisper that sounded frightened. "How am I going to do that?"

"The same way you earned your reputation of being no one to try and take advantage of when you converted those three names your mother gave you into that little three letter name you use now," explained Hoppy, his face showing compassion to everyone in the room.

Hanky and E Jee saw Miss Jab blush.

"Changing Jane Annie Belle into Jab shouldn't make you turn as red as an apple," said Hoppy, his understanding eyes flashing reassurance to Miss Jab. "You must admit that those three names you were known as was quite a mouthful."

"You betcha," chimed in Chats. "I couldn't spit out Jane Annie Belle without stuttering and slobbering all over myself."

Laughter filled the room.

Hoppy pushed his black Stetson slightly back on his head. "Being named after three of the most famous women in the history of the west certainly caught everyone's attention when they found out who you were named after," he said.

Chats began to stutter. "All three of them dare ladies were the toughest, straight shootinest dead eyes that ever lived, by willickers."

All Hanky and E Jee could do was sit and listen. They didn't move.

"Okay," Miss Jab said sheepishly, "I could outshoot most men." She tried to suppress a grin. "Way too many cowboys lost a lot of money finding out the hard way," she continued as her grin won out. "Heck, Hoppy, how do you think I got this here ranch?"

Hoppy and the others joined in adding their assorted smiles.

Hanky and E Jee did not. They were too overwhelmed by what they were hearing.

"Jane Annie Belle, you are some kind of legend," said Hoppy.

E Jee suddenly jumped up and repeated the names Hoppy had just said. "Jane Annie Belle," she said excitedly, her arms going around the waist of Miss Jabs and hugging her. "My name is Jane too," said E Jee to the woman, almost crawling into the back pocket of her jeans. "Jeepers, you have three names just like me. Is Jane your Confirmation name?" she asked. Then she continued on, sputtering like Chats, saying, "Gertrude is my Confirmation name. Gee willickers, I've never heard of any saints by the name of Belle. I know there's a Sainte Ann."

The woman knelt on one knee next to E Jee. "I was never given one of those Confirmation names you mentioned," she said. My parents wanted to protect me from any harm, mainly from the two legged variety like that Ringo fellow. So they named me after three of the toughest, dead eyes in the history of the west." Her head went up and down once. "Did you two young 'uns ever hear of Annie Oakley, Belle Starr and Calamity

Jane?"

Hanky and E Jee looked at Miss Jab, their mouths looking like they were about to swallow their shirts. Of course they had heard of the three famous women of the old west. Every kid who knew how to read a comic book or watch old western movies on television or surf the web knew of them. They continued to stay silent; awe more than respect dictating their silence. Then they heard Hoppy say as he folded his arms across his chest: "Miss Jab I think you're going to need a lot more than three famous names to keep you from being bushwhacked by that Ringo bunch." He looked very serious at the woman. "I think me and my boys might be able to help you get through all of this," he said. He looked around the room at his handful of men. "Boys, I've got a little idea I think might help our good friend, Miss Jab."

Both Hanky and E Jee wondered how Hoppy was going to help. Then they both saw Hoppy look at them as he folded his arms across his chest. "But first, I think what we have to do is to get these two young 'ns back to where they came from."

"You two kids come from Mexico?" asked one of Hoppy's crew, Tim.

"Yep, I think they did," replied Tom, Tim's partner. "The Mexican border is in the direction of where you two kids pointed. Are you sure that's where you came from?"

Hanky and E Jee both nodded, their heads bouncing up and down with gusto. Then they repeated the explanations they had given to Miss Jab and Hoppy earlier about their grandfather and the trip to the Hopalong Cassidy museum in Ohio where they had gone through a large, black velvet drape ending up in front of Miss Jab's corral. "I didn't know so many cattle existed," said E Jee, then stopping to catch her breath as Tim, Tom and the others looked on, Tim and Tom flashing big grins, a couple of times slapping the thigh area of their jeans and letting out howls of laughter along with puffs of dust. Then E Jee started to cry saying: "It's the truth and it's not funny. I miss my mommy and daddy and I don't know if I'll ever see them again."

"Oh, don't pay those two no attention," said Miss Jab stepping alongside of E Jee and putting her arm around her shoulder. "Those two boys laugh when the funeral director, Mister Earp leads his horse drawn hearse up to Boot Hill." She gave E Jee's shoulder a squeeze. "Now dry those pretty tears of yours and I'm sure Mister Cassidy will be able to get you back east to that place called Ohio you came from. If anyone can, Hopalong Cassidy can."

"That's mighty nice of you to say that, Miss Jab and I'll do what I can, said Hoppy. "And I'm sure Chats, Tim, Tom and Randy will be glad to help as well." He looked at his companions, his kind eyes also flashing his request.

"Right you are, Hoppy," said Chats in his low key gravel voice.

"We'll be glad to help, Mister Cassidy," said Tim and Tom in unison, their smiles gone.

"You know you can count on me," said Randy, his handsome face belonging more to a movie star than a cowboy.

"Gentlemen, I thank you," said Hoppy as he looked at Hanky and E Jee. "I know I can count on every one of you."

"You know I'll help," said Miss Jab giving E Jee another reassuring hug. "I think my new lady friend with the three names and I will work pretty darn good together, don't you E Jee?"

"Yes, Miss Jane Annie Belle," said E Jee, her tears now gone.

"And, don't forget me," said Hanky. "I'm not afraid of any cattle rustlers like that Ringo guy. He didn't look so tough to me."

"Well spoken," replied Hoppy mussing the top of Hanky's hair. He looked at Miss Jab. "Do you have any spare Stetsons lying around here? Something that maybe your two kids wore when they were the age of these two," he said. He looked at Hanky and E Jee, smiled and said: "If you two are going to fight bad cowboys, then you'd better look like a couple of real cowboys and not a couple of city slickers from out east." He paused and added. "Didn't you tell me that you were from that big cow town, Chicago?"

Hanky and E Jee gave a single nod.

"Gather around," Hoppy said to the group. "Before our friend, Ringo returns in a nasty mood, we've got to be ready for him," he continued shifting into his business demeanor.

He startled Hanky and E Jee.

"Now here's what I've got in mind," said Hoppy.

Just then they all saw a flash of a light and everyone except E Jee jumped, Miss Jab jumping the most.

"What in tar nation was that?" asked Chats rubbing at his eyes.

"It came from that young 'un there," said Tim nodding in E Jee's directions.

Tom walked over to where E Jee stood looking nervous and unsure of what to do or say. "That flash came from that pink lookin' thing in her hand. I saw it."

Hanky moved alongside of his sister and removed his own iPhone from his pocket and held it up. "E Jee wanted to show all of you a picture of our parents, but she ended up taking a picture of all of you."

"Picture," repeated Randy a polite curiosity in his voice. "Like one of those picture takin' fellows we see every now and then when we're in town?"

"Yeah," said Chats. "That guy keeps duckin' under that black cloth and telling everyone to smile. Sounds kind of stupid to me," he grumbled, the gravel appearing to be growing in his throat.

Miss Jab knelt down on one knew alongside of E Jee. "I'd love to see a picture of your mommy and daddy," she said.

E Jee was overjoyed. She didn't notice everyone else, except her brother give looks to the pink iPhone in her tiny hand as if it were, as Chats muttered to Randy: "That looks like bad Apache medicine to me."

The first day of their grandfather's surprise family vacation to visit the Hopalong Cassidy museum in Cambridge, Ohio wasn't anywhere near what Hanky and E Jee expected. Not by a long shot. What had started out as borderline awful to them had turned into an adventure no one, not one of their friends, no kids they ever knew at school, not even their Grandpa Bucky could come up with. Being lost, meeting a crusty, pretty lady named after Calamity Jane, Annie Oakley and Belle Starr, seeing her two pearl handled six guns and being saved by Hopalong Cassidy and his men was excitement beyond what any Disney writer could possibly create. All of the theme parks of the world together couldn't put together an adventure like they were having. On top of it, they had been made a part of Hoppy's plans to take care of a cattle rustler, cheating gambler and alleged killer who shot his victims in the back, a sidewinder of a thief named, Ringo. Then there were a pair of miniature leather cowboy boots; one held in Hanky's right pocket and the other in E Jee's. More and more magic seemed to come from the boots their grandfather had given them. The more the magic they believed they were experiencing, the harder the boots kicked them. From the moment they had found themselves on the coarse desert sand, they had experienced one close call after another. Neither of the two had been harmed in any way. No kicks were evident now.

After they had all listened to Hoppy's plan, Miss Jab thanked him and then said: "Tonight we celebrated around a camp fire where I'm going to cook up the best beef brisket you cowpokes ever had." She stopped and gave them all a big grin. "Along with the brisket I'm entrusting to Chats who was the best chuck wagon cook in his day, I'm going to prepare a kettle of special pinto beans for you."

The twins sat mesmerized around a hypnotic campfire that seemed to congratulate them on being brave. E Jee's bravery amounted to her taking pictures of the ranch, Hoppy and Topper and a group Selfie where she managed to get the top of her head visible along with all of the new faces she and her brother had met. Those new faces couldn't get over seeing their images come to life on E Jee's iPhone. The pictures had Chats reiterating his feelings about bad Apache medicine and, as much as he tried, he couldn't elude the flash of E Jee's camera. "I ain't smilin' for no flashing picture takin' contraption from up north," he growled to

Tim and Tom before turning his attention back to the smoldering beef brisket.

They had enjoyed Chat's cooking, the brisket cooked on a metal grill that once used to be part of a fence gate that found its way onto Miss Jab's ranch via a handy man she once employed. The handy man kept showing up with all kinds of items. There was a pump handle for the well, a slightly bent pitch fork, even a buggy minus one wheel. The forth wheel showed up a week later looking as if it had been buried in the desert. It had. That's when Miss Jab got more than suspicious and began asking around town looking for information while on her monthly trip for supplies. There had been a rash of thefts, complaints of missing items from private properties and businesses along with barns broken into. Miss Jab put two and two together and it spelled out her handy man's name, Moon. When confronted with what she had found out in town, Moon gave a tip of his seat stained cowboy hat and rode away on a palomino that sported a Skull and Cross Bones brand.

Suddenly Miss Jab tensed up, a look of dismay coloring her face. "That was him," she blurted out getting the attention of the group. "That was Moon mounted alongside of Ringo earlier," she said. Her head went from side to side. "I guess birds of a feather really do flock together."

No one around the campfire doubted what Miss Jab's stated and the explanation that followed. Not even Hoppy. Then they all went back to savoring the meal of beef and beans, Tim and Tom eating almost half of it until Hoppy gave them his, "Manners please, boys" nod.

The remaining brisket and kettle of beans sat off at the edge of the fire resting on the edge of the gate keeping warm. Red hot embers threw off a warmth that took away the growing chill of the desert night. A chunk of fat back set steaming in the middle of the kettle spreading a delicious aroma around the fire. They had eaten from tin plates using their fingers and metal spoons as their eating utensils. Two other new faces had joined them just before they had sat down around the campfire; a pair of cowboys who had rode up to the ranch out of the night. Their names were Roy and Gene and Hoppy and his boys recognized them immediately. There were pats on the back and handshakes all around. Hanky and E Jee weren't a part of the welcoming committee.

Hanky and E Jee had to rub their eyes to believe what they were seeing. "Is it?" asked E Jee.

"Sure is," answered Hanky.

They rubbed their eyes again trying to remove any doubt. The rubbing didn't work, only raising more doubts. Hanky and E Jee found it hard to believe what the two men said to Hoppy about being out on the trail for several days. They related to Hoppy and the others about what they heard about the Ringo incident as they were passing through town and came out to the ranch to see if their old friend, Miss Jab might need a bit of help in the form of a couple of extra cowboys. Ringo was no friend of theirs.

"Those two guys couldn't have been out on the trail for as long as they told Hoppy," said Hanky to E Jee quietly. "They look cleaner than Hoppy on the cover of one of Grandpa Bucky's magazines."

"They do look very clean and neat," E Jee whispered back. "And, they're so very handsome; especially that Roy person."

Then they saw Miss Jab nod toward the front porch of the

ranch house. Off to the side were several spare plates and spoons. "Help yourselves, boys," she said, her own plate showing only a lone uneaten bean. "There's plenty there to go around."

Dinner continued with small talk, especially stories of cattle drives with words like Maverick, Drovers and Mustangs being bandied about by Chats that made everyone laugh especially Tim and Tom. Even Hanky and E Jee laughed, their laughter coming more from listening to the deep gravel voice of Chats.

As the fire was dying down, both Roy and Gene stood up and walked over to where Miss Jabs was sitting on a large mesquite log enjoying her coffee. "Miss Jab," the cowboy name Gene said, "Do you still have those guitars your kids used to play?"

"I do," she replied, nodding toward the front door of the house. "You'll find them in there."

"You did say there were two," said Roy following Gene into the house.

"That I did," said Miss Jab. "Almost as good as new as the day I bought them as Christmas presents for the boys."

The two newest members of the group were back sitting around the fire with the others tuning up the guitars.

"Yah, ready, Roy?" asked Gene.

Roy strummed the strings of his guitar. "Ready as I'll ever be."

Hanky and E Jee sat amazed at what they were witnessing. "It's just like an old cowboy movie," said Hanky to his sister. They both listened in total silence, almost afraid to move a muscle. The singing cowboy duo was another surprise event that they couldn't wait to tell their Grandfather about and E Jee was quick to put her camera into action, the flash not seeming to have an effect on any members of the group, not even the two new faces strumming the guitars and singing.

The singing came to an abrupt end when Chats tried to sing, *Get along Little Doggie* solo. It was then that Hoppy, Miss Jab, Tim and Tom and Randy stretched and yawned. Both Roy and Gene got the message and almost immediately strummed a final chord on their guitars leaving Chats in a mid, "get along."

"We all had a big day," said Hoppy to the group. "And, tomorrow's going to be an even bigger day." His arms stretched out; "Time for some shuteye, he said." He glanced at Miss Jab. "Do you have a place for these two easterners to bed down?" he asked, the glowing embers of the fire highlighting his contagious smile.

"They can use the beds in my kid's room," she said. She glanced at Hoppy. "You and the boys can bed down in the old bunk house out back. I've got some clean blankets I can get for all of you."

"Much obliged," said Hoppy as the others nodded their appreciation. He walked over to where Hanky and E Jee stood enthralled with what had gone on. Nervous anticipation rushed through them about what lie ahead. In no particular order was sleeping in Miss Jab's ranch house located somewhere near Mexico and in what was named the Arizona Territory. "You two will sleep safe and sound tonight with Miss Jab looking out for you," said Hoppy, his reassuring smile and eyes never changing their message. "Come the morning, I'll see what I can do about locating your parents." Hoppy paused, his smile now gone. "You did mention a couple of places where your folks might be as I recall." He gave a nod and asked, "Chicago or Ohio, right?"

Chapter 8

"You two should be right comfy under those covers," said Miss Jab as she pulled up the sheet and blanket under E Jee's chin. She turned to Hanky and said: "You're a big boy. "You don't need no tuckin' in."

"Yes, Mam," replied Hanky. "And, thanks for letting me and E Jee sleep here in the house with you."

"You're welcome," said Miss Jab as she bent over to blow out the kerosene lamp on the small table located between the two narrow beds. "You two be sure and stay under the covers, you hear. The desert night can get mighty chilly." She smiled and then doused the lamp. She walked to the bedroom door, turned and said to them:

"Now don't you come a wakin' me up if you hear the coyotes howlin' during the night. They're just singin' you two a lullaby. Kind of like Roy and Gene was tryin' to do before Chats had to go an ruin it."

Both Hanky and E Jee giggled. Then the door closed and the room went black.

"Are you still here, Hanky?" asked E Jee her voice showing she was scared.

"I'm right here," said Hanky. "Where'd you think I'd be?" He let out a giggle. "I'm not about to go outside and meet up with no coyotes, as Miss Jab called them or, worse yet, that bad guy, Ringo and his gang. Man, now that was a scary looking bunch."

"I don't want to talk about them," said E Jee, sleep starting to take her over. "I just want us to be with mommy and daddy."

Hanky rolled over on his side to avoid a lump in the mattress and saw a glow coming from E Jee's bed. "Don't worry," he said trying to be the reassuring protective brother, "Hoppy said he'd help us and I know he will. And, beside, maybe tomorrow you'll be able to get a signal on your cell phone. You can try and call mom and dad; maybe even send them some of the pictures we took today." He paused and yawned. "Especially a picture of Hoppy," followed his yawn. "Boy, would Grandpa Bucky ever be surprised." Hanky yawned again. "Now turn off that phone light and save your battery. If you didn't notice, there ain't a wall around here that has an electric plug." He paused and then added: "Do you think that maybe Miss Jab doesn't have any electricity way out here in the middle of all this sand?"

The room turned silent, the quiet lasting for a minute; the minute seeming like an hour. Then E Jee said: "Hanky is that man really Hopalong Cassidy?"

Hanky rolled over on his back and placed his hands behind his head. "He looks like him," he said. "We all heard everyone here call him Hoppy or Mister Cassidy, didn't we?"

"I guess," said E Jee, feeling unsure.

"If he said he was Hoppy and everyone called him that, then, well, he's got to be Hopalong Cassidy." There was silence and then Hanky let out a loud laugh. "Oh, boy is Grandpa Bucky ever going to be surprised when we tell him about out our meeting the real Hopalong Cassidy." He laughed louder. "Can you see Grandpa Bucky's face when we tell him we ate beef brisket and pinto beans with his hero?" He let out another long yawn. "Maybe we can get Hoppy to be in a picture with just the two of us," he said his voice showing his excitement. "Now that would make Grandpa Bucky really jealous."

E Jee joined in the laughter. "Gee willickers would he ever be," she said. Then she let out a loud laugh, took a deep breath and said, "And the beans made him fart."

They both laughed hysterically until they heard Miss Jab's voice.

"You two pipe down in there!" she hollered. "I'm tryin' to get some sleep."

Sleep didn't come easy to Hanky and E Jee. They were first serenaded by a pack of howling coyotes that seemed to use their names in their haunting cries that echoed well into the night. "Did you hear that?" asked E Jee in a whisper when she first heard the cries echoing across the valley.

"I heard," said Hanky. He didn't whisper.

They both pulled their bed covers up to just below their eyes and lay frozen like two blocks of ice. The coyotes' cries continued, their wailing filling the pitch black desert night making it sound, as Hanky remembered, the night their teenage neighbor, Frankie Lavecio had a party at his house while his parents were away for the weekend visiting his ailing grandmother. The ear splitting music combined with adolescent yells and screams fueled by alcoholic beverages furnished by Frankie's twenty one year old brother, Guido kept Hanky and the entire Goodson family up past midnight. That's when Hanky and E Jee's father got out of bed, dressed and went next door. No one except their father and Guido Lavecio knew what transpired at the front door of the Lavecio residence, but the house was suddenly vacated as if a bomb threat had been received. Stumbling teenagers, like rats abandoning a sinking ship, scurried in all directions leaving the two Lavecio boys turning off the loud music and switching off all the lights. The next morning Hanky and E Jee's father sat at the kitchen table sipping his coffee with his left hand, his right covered by a dish towel filled with ice. Since it was summer and sunny, no one ever asked why Guido Lavecio wore his sunglasses during the next week twenty four hours a day.

Just when E Jee was thinking about crawling out of her bed and joining her brother in his for safety, the coyotes put their serenading to sleep for the night. Both Hanky and E Jee lay perfectly still, listening, their ears straining. They heard nothing. Then sleep overtook them. It didn't take their dreams long to set in.

E Jee tossed and turned most of the night until she felt herself shivering as if she were in a blizzard. That's when she woke up, her teeth chattering. It was still almost totally dark out; a quarter moon finding a sanctuary behind a bank of clouds that had drifted in from the southwest. E Jee quickly discovered why she was shivering. Her sheet and blanket were wrapped around her neck and head; her bare feet numb from the cold making her feel that she had just walked home from school in the dead of winter. It didn't take her long to roll up in her covers and get warm. It also didn't take long for the dream about her parents to return. In the morning she felt she had been crying most of the night because she was homesick and missed her parents. Her first try at calling them on her cell phone got a, "No service" message on her screen.

"Stupid thing," she muttered to the phone as she gave it a shake. "You always work at home," she said irritated. "Why not here in Ohio?" she asked. She looked at her brother who was wrapped up in his blanket. "Hanky," she said in a whisper. "We are in Ohio aren't we?"

Hanky's answer was a sound that resembled a mumble.

Hanky, too, was having a dream. His was an ongoing saga of his getting Hopalong Cassidy out of one jam or another, mostly with Ringo and his gang. Hoppy, as Hanky knew, didn't like violence and using guns. The only time Hoppy ever used his guns was in self defense and, because he was an expert shot, his aim sent a bullet into the gun the bad guy was pointing at him. Hoppy held the record for shooting more guns out of more hands of bad cowboys in the entire southwest. Hanky was always there by Hoppy's side in his dreams. He was another set of eyes for Hoppy, always warning him when extra men showed up out of Hoppy's sight. Hanky would have his official Hopalong Cassidy pistols at the ready. When needed he would fire off a warning shot to alert Hoppy. The warning shot was always the noise of a cap, a roll loaded in his pistols; the shot loud enough to give Hoppy a chance to protect himself. That night Hanky woke up sweating, his eyes searching to no avail in the dark room for Ringo's men who had surrounded Miss Jab's ranch house. "Hoppy," he said to the blackened room, "Hoppy, I'm sorry." He choked back a sob. "I didn't mean to run out of caps for my pistols." Hanky looked and saw the first sign of daylight out of the dusty and streaked bedroom window. He sighed and realized he had been dreaming. Then he glanced at E Jee and thought she was sleeping soundly. He sighed again, rolled himself up in the covers and dozed off.

Hanky wasn't asleep long when he heard the bedroom door creak open. His brain had him tensing up as he heard someone enter the room, the floor boards moaning ever so softly. He slowly opened his eyes and could see someone standing in between his bed and E Jee's. Then his heart almost exploded.

"Time to rise and shine, you two magpies," a voice said.

The voice belonged to Miss Jab. "You two got some chores to do before breakfast," she said as if giving them an order like their father would. She looked at E Jee. "You, Missy, you're goin' out to the hen house and collect a big basket of eggs. That bunch out in the bunk house will have growlin' stomachs this morning."

E Jee's eyes grew the size of silver dollars as she replied: "Really?" Her eyes stayed wide open. "But, Miss Jab, I never collected eggs before. Will those chickens bite me?"

Miss Jab wanted to smile, but didn't. Her eyes, however, did. "Missy, you'll learn real fast how to snatch up an egg without getting your hand pecked by some unhappy hen," she said her head going slowly from side to side. "And, if those chickens peck at you, why you just peck 'em right back," she instructed. Then she turned her attention to Hanky. "I think it's time a big boy like you learned how to milk a few cows."

Hanky had pulled his jeans just over his knees and he could feel his tongue racing toward the bottom of his stomach. "But...." He never got a chance to finish because Miss Jab stopped him with her right hand, palm up, extended in front of her.

"Save your breath for workin'," she said. "You and your

sister chatted enough last night to last you two life times. Now finish pullin' your britches up," she ordered as she turned her attention back to E Jee. "And, you, Sleeping Beauty get yourself dressed pronto. I'll meet you both in the hen house." She turned and walked out of the tiny bedroom.

Hanky looked at his sister, a bewildered look on his face, his sleepy eyes coated with the Sandman's handiwork. "Grandpa Bucky ain't ever gonna believe us."

E Jee had been frightened at first when walking amidst the squawking hens and their reluctance to let her take eggs. Miss Jab's lesson at egg gathering was simple and swift. One quick, but gentle swat with one hand had the hen off her nest while her other hand snatched up what was in the nest. The egg quickly found its way into a large woven basket with a big loop handle. In an instant, E Jee found herself following Miss Jab's instructions. Her first swat was more like her hand fanning at the air and the hen that had met her hand gave her what appeared to be a nasty look before letting out a squawk and not budging. The hen did more than budge when E Jee's second swat carried more authority; way too much authority. Not only did the hen move, but the commotion she caused had several others vacating their roosts. E Jee jumped right in and snatched up egg after egg. When she had finished she had collected somewhere over three dozen eggs, breaking only two slightly. She didn't want to stop until she saw Miss Jab stick her head into the hen house, glance at the basket and then give E Jee a congratulatory shake of her head, indicating that she should follow her back to the ranch house. E Jee noticed that Miss Jab was carrying a pail in one hand. Inside the pail looked like milk. "Did my brother do that" she asked?

"Kind of," said Miss Jab without turning to look back at E Jee.

"My brother really milked a cow?" she asked.

Miss Jab nodded and let out a grumble. "It took your brother some time, but he finally got the hang of it once he got kicked by the cow he was trying to milk. He'll have a good bruise but it won't be long before it'll clear up." She smiled at E Jee. "I sent him with Tim and Tom to be sure that my new calves were taken care of. Like I said, your brother is a slow learner. Maybe a kick or two from some frisky calves will smartin' him up. If that don't work, I'm sure Tim and Tom can teach him a lesson or two." She laughed.

E Jee found herself liking the woman named Miss Jab more and more. When she got back to the ranch house kitchen and set down her basket of eggs on a table next to a huge black, cast iron, wood burning stove, she was eager to continue helping Miss Jab. "What would you like me to do next?" she asked politely.

Miss Jab nodded toward a set of cabinets opposite the cook stove. "You'll find some plates and cups on the left side of the cabinet. Get out eight of each." She stopped and thought a minute. "No, make that ten. No tellin' what Mister Cassidy has up his sleeve for today and no tellin' who else might show up."

E Jee scurried back and forth between the cabinet and the long ranch house dining room table in the big living room area that doubled as a dining room when Miss Jab had to feed the extra drovers she hired for a cattle drive. E Jee set out ten white plates spacing them evenly around the table. Ten white coffee cups followed. She had tried to remember what her mother had taught her about setting a table. Did the cups go on the right or the left? She chose right and then remembered her mother's instructions. She went back into the kitchen and was greeted by aromas that made her tiny stomach growl and her nose wrinkle with pleasure. "Oh, Miss Jab," she said, "does that ever smell yummy."

"Yummy," repeated Miss Jab as she looked over her shoulder and smiled at E Jee. "That must be one of those new fangled eastern words." She nodded at the cabinets where E Jee had taken the plates and cups. "In that big drawer on the right you'll find the eatin' utensils. There should be enough for everyone."

E Jee didn't waste a second. She wanted to impress Miss Jab with doing a fast job, but found that she could only carry half the knives, forks and spoons that were needed, a couple falling to the floor.

"Pick them up on your second trip," said Miss Jab without taking her attention away from the stove and the cast iron skillets that were emitting spitting sounds along with filling the kitchen with, according to E Jee, yummy smells. "Just wipe 'em off on your jeans and set 'em on the table. The guys'll never know the difference. A little dirt never hurt anybody," she continued. "I used to tell my boys when they was younger than you and your brother, that we lived by the five second rule when anything fell on the floor. If a fork, a slice of bread or whatever got dropped, there was no way some dirt or some bug could get on it that fast. I'd tell them to pick it up, wipe it off and eat it or eat with it." She paused as if reflecting then said: "Not a one of them ever came down with a danged thing."

E Jee finished setting the table after having had to change the layout of the knives, forks and spoons, switching the forks to the left side of the plates after realizing her mistake. "I don't want Mommy to be mad at me because I caused her an embarrassment," she said to the dining room table and her efforts before returning to the kitchen and the growing yummy smells. "Is there anything else you want me to do, Miss Jab?" she asked politely.

Miss Jab didn't waste a second. "See that trap door in the floor you're almost standing on?" she asked. "That leads to the root cellar where I keep some of our food from spoiling. Open it up and then get that kerosene lamp over there on the table, light it if you think know how and go down in the cellar and bring up that big bowl of butter and that jar of prickly pear jam."

"Prickly pear?" repeated E Jee.

"It's a jam I make out of cactus," replied Miss Jab without taking her attention from what she was now doing at the stove. "After you bring that stuff up for me then I've got a real fun job for you. Oh, boy, will your brother ever be jealous of you."

"Gee willickers, what is it, Miss Jab?"

E Jee couldn't believe what she had done. After learning how to strike a sulfur wooden match and light a kerosene lamp, she had discovered what a root cellar was and surprised at how cool the temperature was from that of the ranch house and especially outside in the desert heat. Her chores in the house were done. She had the table set after she had put out salt and pepper shakers and Miss Jab had relieved her frustration of not finding any paper napkins because there were no such things, her eyes turned silver dollar sizes again.

"Take one of those chairs out on the porch," Miss Jab had said to her as E Jee waited in the kitchen. She had done what she had been instructed and stood by the chair near the open front door waiting for Miss Jab's next instructions.

It didn't take Miss Jab long to join her on the porch. What E Jee noticed immediately was that the lady was carrying what looked like a magic wand. The wand wasn't magic nor was it a wand. Only shaped like one, a bit thicker, but about as long and rusty. The wand was a piece of iron rod and Miss Jab handed it to E Jee who looked at the wand, her face full of curiosity, and then looked back at Miss Jab.

Miss Jab's glance traveled up.

E Jee saw it immediately. Miss Jab was looking at a black metal triangle shaped object suspended from the front porch overhang by what looked like a two foot length of barbed wire. The legs of the triangle were about a foot each. Miss Jab nodded at the chair next to E Jee. "Take that chair of yours and position it under that there triangle," she said, her nod directed at the triangle. "Now, be careful and get up on that chair and stand just off to the side of that triangle," she continued to instruct. "When I tell you, I want you to take that steel bar you have in your hand and place it in that opening of that metal triangle. Then I want you to use that metal bar to hit all of the sides of that triangle as hard and as fast as you can. Understand?"

E Jee nodded and got up on the chair getting into position just as she had been told. She looked at Miss Jab waiting for her next instructions.

"One other thing, E Jee," said Miss Jab. "When you're hitting that triangle," she said pausing, then interjecting: "By the way, that's our dinner bell." There was another pause. "When you're hitting that triangle as hard and as fast as you can, you shout out as loud as you can, 'Come and get it' and then watch and see what happens."

E Jee watched Miss Jab disappear into the house and knew she was going to the kitchen. The yummy smells couldn't get any yummier and then she heard Miss Jab yell: "The vittles are ready and its eatin' time," she hollered! "Ring that bell!"

E Jee attacked the metal triangle with a vengeance. She was so excited she almost fell off the chair as she swung the metal rod. Her furious swings seemed to go in a million different directions at once. She couldn't believe what she saw next. At first, she thought she was under attack by Ringo's gang. Men came running from every which direction and that included her brother and Hoppy. There were also two others who joined Hoppy's crew. E Jee could only stare, the metal wand clutched in her hand while the men raced up the wooden stairs, their boots pounding like the thundering hooves of the horses that had sent her and her brother racing for the ranch house the day before.

Hanky sat next to his sister at the far end of the table and away from Miss Jab and the two new visitors who Hoppy had brought in to join them. "I didn't believe it when I saw them," said Hanky.

"They can't be real," whispered E Jee back to Hanky out of the corner of her mouth.

"They look real to me," said Hopalong Cassidy down at the other end of the table looking directly at Hanky and E Jee, shocking them both.

Hanky and E Jee turned beet red and everyone at the table laughed including the two additional members who had joined them. Neither Hanky nor E Jee could speak.

It was Hoppy who eased the embarrassment of the brother and sister. "You know, when I was your age," he began, "I would always get embarrassed and feel strange around new faces," he said, then taking a pause as he looked at the two men sitting across the table from him. "Okay," he started out trying not to smile, "I must admit that an Indian joining us for one of Miss Jab's great home cooked breakfasts is not an everyday thing." He stopped and smiled at Miss Jab. "And, I know, the first time my cowboy friend here," he said nodding at the man seated next to him, "joined us to share in a plate of beef hide and beans around a campfire after a tough day on the trail, the mask he wore did cause Miss Jab some concern."

"It really is him," blurted out E Jee. "I don't believe it."

"Do you think I should holler out, 'Hi-ho, Silver'" said the man across from Hoppy who was wearing a black mask concealing his eyes.

Everyone at the table laughed, Tim and Tom slapping the wooden table top so hard the plates and utensils jumped.

Hanky and E Jee didn't laugh. They couldn't believe they were in the company of the Lone Ranger and Tonto.

"Are you really the Lone Ranger?" asked Hanky in awe, his sister staring as if she were a bronze statue.

"I don't see anyone else wearing a mask at the table," he said seriously so as not to offend Hanky and E Jee. "Just look at my mask as another article of clothing. It's what I wear. It's how people recognize me." He smiled politely at the two. "There are those who don't recognize me at all unless I'm with my good friend and companion, Tonto."

"It is you," said E Jee, her excitement growing. "And, it's Tonto. Gee willickers, Tonto. Oh, my, golly gee." She pushed her chair away from the table then caught herself and looked at Miss Jab. "Miss Jab," she said ever so polite, "may I get up from the table so I can meet Mister Tonto and the Lone Ranger?"

Tonto and Lone Ranger stood up as if on cue, the Lone Ranger saying: "How 'bout if Tonto and I come down and sit by you?"

E Jee stood motionless. Her head was the only part of her that moved, it going up and down in slow motion.

"And, how's about I get that pot of coffee off the stove?" said Miss Jab standing up. "You folks look like you could use an eye opener."

They all heard it at the same time, each reacting differently. It was definitely a gunshot followed instantly by a window pane shattering. Then there was the sound from Miss Jab, her left hand going up to the top of her right shoulder, a look on her face not of pain, but of anger. She gave a muffled cry of, "Oh," before dropping to her knees and pushing E Jee with her. "Get down, Hanky," she hollered out.

The words hadn't cleared her lips when Hanky found himself diving under the table. "Geez, Miss Jab," he said. "There's blood on your shoulder."

"Ah, they just winged me," said Miss Jab as she examined the slight tear in her blouse at the shoulder, the area turning red. It's just a flesh wound. I'll be alright." She looked at E Jee who was under the table with Hanky. "E Jee," she said calmly. "Crawl on the floor over to that far cabinet. In there you'll find a first-aid kit I put together to handle emergencies that might happen here. Being a rancher can sometimes be dangerous." She let out a laugh. "I never knew it would be this dangerous." She paused as she watched E Jee crawl across the floor without once questioning Miss Jab's request. She was back in second with the box. "Good girl, E Jee," she said taking the box from her and removing a bottle marked, Iodine along with several rolls of bandages.

Hanky and E Jee just stared and didn't know what to do except stay under the table because the number of gunshots had increased during that first minute. Shattered window glass flew in a million different directions, most of it raining down on the floor. Splinters of wood from the door and window frames poked out, the bullets that did the splintering now buried in the opposite wall. So much had happened neither of them realized that Hoppy's plan from the night before had gone into operation.

Hoppy's men operated like a synchronized machine, sprinting to their designated spots that had been outlined the night before.

Tim and Tom, guns drawn, threw open the back door. The door quickly sported several new splintered holes. Tim and Tom had expected the gun fire. Now they knew where the shooters were located. Tim with both of his guns blazing fire kept the gun men down. Tom was out the door and behind a rain barrel for protection. Both of his guns began firing when he saw the first sign of a hat. When that happened Tim was out the door and headed for the opposite side of the ranch house from where his partner was firing. He took cover behind a long wooden watering trough that was used earlier by the horses. They were now tied up in the barn behind the house. He had a perfect view of the two assailants who were shooting. He cocked his two pistols and let loose with a volley of fire.

"I'm hit," screamed one of the men grabbing at his arm, his gun falling to the ground. His partner didn't respond. He had also taken a bullet and lay motionless. Tim gave Tom a nod indicating that he would cover him as he went up where the two men had been hiding. As Tom drew closer he gave a wave to Tim to move forward.

"By golly," said Tim to Tom as they looked at the two gunshot victims. "Them two aren't any older than Hanky."

"Darned Ringo," muttered Tom. "He's gone out and hired children to fight his battles. "I know Hoppy don't like no bloodshed, but if I get Ringo in my sights, he'll have more holes in him than that wool blanket Miss Jab gave me to sleep on last night."

As Tim and Tom were tying up the two wounded gunmen as if they had hog tied a couple of run-a-way calves, Chats has laid down a volley of gun fire from his lever action thirty-thirty so that Randy could vault over the front porch railing. He looked as if he were flying as his boots hit the ground barely kicking up any dust and headed in a crouch for the main gate of the corral. Randy had spotted a couple of Ringo's rustlers among the cattle and knew they were about to open the gate and stampede the cattle.

The cattle were more than ready to run for it what with the amount of gunfire exploding around them. As Randy sprinted toward the corral gate, bullets were kicking up the sandy ground around him. He had counted Chats' shots and took a dive landing just behind the corral gate on the last one. Giving Chats time to reload, he began to shoot at what he knew were a pair of cowboy boots. His aim was careful and accurate. He did not want to hit any of the cattle and his aim continued to be true as he shot the heel off of one of the boots he saw. Out of the corner of his eye he saw a pair of rusted spurs. Two quick well aimed shots had the spurs lying on the dusty ground. "Shoot at a lady, will ya," he muttered. Then he heard Chats begin firing again and he quickly reloaded his pistols.

While the shooting was going on, Hoppy, the Lone Ranger and Tonto had worked their way behind the corral and entered the barn where all of their horses were. Before entering the barn door, Hoppy gave a signal to the Lone Ranger and Tonto to get into position where they could see inside the barn. He knew that Ringo would have at least one of his gang stationed inside. When the Lone Ranger and Tonto were in position, Hoppy walked into the barn as if he were going to clean out the stalls. He walked into four guns, a pair in each of the hands of two of Ringo's men.

"Guess this ain't your lucky day, Cassidy," said one of the men, a scowl on his face, both of his pistols cocked and aimed at Hoppy's heart.

The other man spit a wad of chewing tobacco juice on the straw covered ground. His guns were also pointed at Hoppy and he waved them back and forth as if taunting Hoppy.

Hoppy surprised the men by folding his arms across his chest. "You gentlemen should learn that your boss, Ringo, isn't a man to be trusted," he said as if he were having a friendly conversation with the two men who were about to end his life. "Now, if he would've told you everything there was to know about how to rustle cattle from an innocent woman, he would not have set you up to spend a lot of years in jail." Hoppy paused and smiled at both men. "That is, if this is a lucky day for the both of you." He kept on smiling and the two men started to get nervous. "You could be spending the rest of eternity in Boot Hill north of town. "I'm sure Mr. Earp the undertaker would really appreciate the business."

The man who spit out the chewing tobacco juice had some of it now running down his chin. "How you gonna put us in jail, Cassidy when you're gonna be pushin' up daisies?"

"Because Mister Cassidy won't be pushing up any daisies, white man," came a voice from behind them.

"I wouldn't turn around if I were you," said another voice from behind the two men.

They never expected to be caught by surprise and looked at one another their eyes questioning what they should do next. Before they could react there was a whirling noise in the barn. Actually it was a pair of whirling noises as two lariats flew through the air, each landing over the heads of the men. Before they realized, they were being yanked to the ground and tied up.

"Looks like you haven't lost any of your ropin' skills, Tonto."

"I don't believe it," said the man with the tobacco juice on his chin. He choked and promptley swallowed his chewing tobacco.

"What in blazes are you two doing here?" asked the other man feeling his wrists tied behind him and then those same wrists tie to a rope around his ankles.

"Helping friends," said the Lone Ranger. "That's what one good citizen does for another good citizen who's in need. Didn't your boss, Ringo teach you that?"

Hanky and E Jee heard the gun shots but didn't fully understand that the ranch was under attack. Ringo and his gang of outlaws were in the process of rustling Miss Jab's cattle as well as ending her life and the lives of the others who were at the ranch to help her. What Hanky and E Jee didn't realize was that their lives were also in jeopardy. Both Hanky and E Jee wanted to go to the window for a better look but Miss Jab wouldn't let them saying: "Stay down you two. One of us taking a bullet today is one too many." She looked at E Jee. "Can I trust you not to get shot if I ask you to crawl over to the sink and bring me a drink of water?"

E Jee knew Miss Jab wasn't joking about getting shot. She stayed down and crawled to where the water pitcher was on the kitchen counter. To be extra careful, E Jee grabbed hold of the counter top with both hands and slowly pulled herself up until her eyes were looking at and through the filled water pitcher. She could see through the kitchen window, the lone pane of glass not broken by flying bullets, but the water in the pitcher distorted her vision. She was hoping to get a glimpse of what was going on outside. Her eyes searched for the corral but her vision was blocked by something that looked like a hideous Halloween mask resembling a zombie that her brother wore the year before for Trick or Treating. The mask covered the entire window. The mask became more than a trick and definitely not a treat. It turned out to be real life; that life in the form of Ringo's face, his frightening eyes saying, "Ah, ha, I got you." E Jee did the only thing she could think of. She let out a blood curdling scream and crawled back in the direction of Miss Jab so fast her hands and knees didn't touch the floor. It wasn't fast enough.

The door exploded open and two of Ringo's men pounced on E Jee and Hanky before they knew what happened. Miss Jab didn't even have time to go for her gun, her good hand putting pressure on her wound, because Ringo had pulled her up by her short, curly blond hair.

"I told you them cattle was mine, lady," snarled Ringo. He let out a nasty laugh. "Now, if you don't mind, I'm taking these two young 'uns for a bit of insurance."

One of Ringo's men had both hands and arms around a kicking and squirming Hanky who kept wondering why he didn't think of wearing spurs with his cowboy boots. His kicking and fighting went for naught as he found himself being tied up with what looked like a lasso. He could see the same thing was happening to E Jee. She looked almost comical fighting her captor. Before they knew it, they were being carried out of the ranch house both hearing what sounded like the kitchen table collapsing in a crash and a moan coming from Miss Jab. They never had a chance to look back as they found themselves lying on their stomachs across the necks of two horses, coils of tight rope wrapped around their bodies from almost head to toe. Then the galloping and bouncing started and they couldn't scream. They didn't have the breath to even whimper.

As Ringo and the remainder of his gang rode off, Hoppy and the others were herding the part of Ringo's gang they had captured to the ranch house. They saw a half dozen horses galloping off but didn't see Hanky and E Jee draped over the necks of two of the horses.

"Runnin' away like the cowards they are," growled Chats as he looked down the sights of his Winchester and frustrated that they he didn't have a shot.

"Miss Jab, are you alright?" asked Hoppy as he saw the wounded woman on her knees and trying to get up from the remains of the kitchen table that was in a dozen broken pieces.

"They took the kids," she said the look on her face stating that she had somehow failed to protect Hanky and E Jee. "It all happened so fast, Hoppy," she blurted out. "Ringo and his boys were in and out of here so fast I didn't know what happened." She pointed at her shoulder and the blood stain on her blouse. "I never got a chance to go for my guns."

Easy, Miss Jab," said Hoppy as he started to check the wound in her shoulder. "Looks like the bullet just creased you. It looks like a bad scratch, but it should heal quickly and you shouldn't have a scar."

"I know someone who's gonna have a scar if I ever catch up with him," she said.

"We all want to contribute to that scar," said Hoppy. "And, I know just how we're gonna do it." He looked at the others his eyes staying a second on each pair of eyes in the group in front of him. "Listen carefully," he said in his usual calm soft spoken manner. "Now here's what we're going to do."

Chapter 9

Both Hanky and E Jee felt as if their insides had been pushed out of their spines from the bouncing they had taken as the horses galloped as fast as the riders could spur them on. Then, after what seemed an eternity of being punched in the stomach, the horses came to a trot and then a slow walk; finally they stopped. Hanky and E Jee felt relief, but only for a moment. The next thing they knew they each felt a pair of hands grab them by the shirt collar and belt. Then they were being flung off the horse they were on. They hit the sand and rocky ground landing on their backsides like a couple of bales of hay being dropped from the loft of Miss Jab's barn. Both felt the wind knocked out of their lungs and they gasped for air.

"That woman's cattle will soon be ours and that ranch of hers, like her, will be no more," they heard Ringo state as they tried to catch their breath. "When we get back to her ranch we'll burn it to the ground with her in it," he stated.

Before Hanky and E Jee could recover from the shock of what happened to them they heard the horses gallop away. Ringo's threat about what he was going to do Miss Jab, her ranch and her cattle penetrating the fog in their heads.

E Jee had become more mad than scared. She was mad that she couldn't help Miss Jab when the men broke into the kitchen of the ranch house. Her anger grew at how useless her kicking, arm swinging and trying to bite her assailant had become. She had been like a playful toy in the man's strong, harsh grip. Now she felt more than useless and even madder wound up by the coils of rope and lying discarded on the ground lie a piece of trash. Then she could feel her courage return as she remembered what her Grandpa Bucky had said about God not making any trash.

Hanky, too, was angry. He knew the heels of his boots had caught his assailant on the shins, but was dumfounded that there wasn't a cry of pain. Ringo's man seemed to crush his ribs the more he kicked and squirmed. Now he was lying on the ground next to his sister bound up and looking off to the side to see the horses disappear. He turned his head and looked into the face of a giant tumble weed that had stopped tumbling when it ran into Hanky's head. Hanky shook his head violently and the tumble weed continued to amble on. His eyes then picked up the sight of some sage brush and tiny clumps of Teddy Bear Cholla cactus. Hanky started laughing, his laughter startling E Jee.

"How can you find anything to laugh at, Dufus," she said.

Just as the riders spurred their horses he could only see them from the knees down. After they had ridden off, Hanky realized that two of the men had no heels on their boots. They looked like they had been shot off. When he told that to his sister she began to giggle.

E Jee felt her fear grow for the safety of Miss Jab. Over-hearing parts of Ringo's plan also had her fearing for the safety of Hoppy and his men. But, somehow, she just knew that the Lone Ranger and Tonto would come to their aid. She also remembered Hoppy talking about trust to her and her brother when he was formulating his plan and sharing it with them. She trusted that he would get them out of the predicament they were in. Something bigger, however, bothered E Jee as she lay hurting on the ground feeling that every bone in her tiny body had been rearranged after being dumped off the horse. She knew that she had seen Ringo before. Then it dawned on her. He was the man in the office at the Hopalong Cassidy Museum that had shoved her and her brother through the black velvet curtain.

Hoppy had quickly come up with a new plan to save Miss Jab, her ranch and cattle. It was simple, brief and consisted of two parts. The first part was for Tim and Tom to take Ringo's men they had captured to town and turn them into the sheriff. Once the sheriff had them locked up, he was to form a posse and follow Tim and Tom to Miss Jab's ranch. At the ranch, they would position several members of the posse in the barn's loft so they would have a clear line of fire at the perimeter of the corral. The other members would stay on horseback inside ready for a signal from Hoppy to come galloping out of the barn to surprise Ringo and his gang.

Tim and Tom carried out their responsibility. They stacked hay bales in front of the ranch house. Their job was to position themselves under the front porch using the hay bales for protection. They had but one target and that was Ringo. Hoppy and the others would join them carrying out the rest of his plan to put Ringo and his gang away.

The second part of the plan involved inviting Ringo and his men into a trap. The ranch had to look like it was vacant except for the cattle. They would appear to be waiting for Ringo and his men to take them away. This part of the plan was tricky and, if it didn't go off perfectly, it could cost Hoppy his life.

To prevent endangering Hoppy, the rest of his men were to stay out of sight. Chats would be positioned in the ranch house. To bait the trap, Chats would leave the ranch house door wide open. Ringo and his men would never see him resting on one knee beneath the window next to the open door, his Winchester cocked and ready.

Tonto and the Lone Ranger would be hidden in a clump of Organ Pipe cacti, Silver and Scout at the ready.

"Are you sure you're going to be alright?" Hoppy asked Miss Jab after he had spelled out his plan. He had redressed her wound and felt bad that she was on the receiving end of a bullet that had been meant for him.

"I'm just fine," she said. "The moment you and your boys leave here I'm going to fasten a couple of horses to my old buckboard and head out to look for those two kids."

"Be careful, Miss Jab," said Hoppy. "Ringo's the kind of rustler that operates without a heart in his chest. He'd just as soon see you dead than not, and he's determined to get that herd of yours one way or another." He gave her a serious look. "Don't you go after those two kids unarmed, you hear," he warned pointing at her guns, the pearl handles gleaming and waiting to be grabbed from the holsters. "You know how I don't use mine unless I'm forced into it," he said. "A man with no soul like, Ringo, well, he won't give you a chance to be forced. He'll plug you and then ask questions later." Hoppy paused looking way too serious. "I just hope those two youngsters haven't been harmed."

Miss Jab watched Hoppy and the others ride off in a different direction than the one Ringo had taken. She knew that Ringo would get rid of Hanky and E Jee in the desert and then take a straight line route to his run down ranch where a reinforcement of thieves and cutthroats waited. The sting of the gunshot wound had her dander up as she walked to the barn. Ignoring the pain as best she could, she hitched up her two favorite horses, Apple and Pie to her weathered buckboard. The hitching went slower than she wanted, the pain in her shoulder refusing to be ignored and telling her to take it easy and even rethink what she was doing. Her own plan was well calculated and based on one fact—Ringo wasn't about to be weighed down by the extra weight of two more riders no matter how small or light they might be. He would leave his hostages out in the desert and if they didn't survive, well, so be it.

Once she had gotten herself seated on the old buckboard bench, she placed her own Winchester lever action rifle along alongside of her; both pistols were holstered and she positioned a third six shooter under the bench behind her feet. She knew that Ringo would shoot first and ask questions later. She wasn't about to give him that option.

Hanky and E Jee couldn't believe what had just happened to them. They lay on the ground looking in the direction where a slowly disappearing cloud of dust that had been created by Ringo and his men riding off had disappeared. Neither said a word, both realizing that they were being left behind. What was worse is that they were still wrapped up in coils of rope, their hands tied behind their backs and laying defenseless on the rock and cactus covered ground.

"Do you think they'll come back for us," asked E Jee as she bounced and squirmed on the ground to turn and face her brother?

"I don't think so," said Hanky feeling the tightness of the large, clumsy knot binding his wrists together slipping and sliding, digging into his skin.

The twins, especially E Jee, were frustrated that they couldn't get at their cell phones. They had put the phones in their back pockets just before they went out to do their chores for Miss Jab and forgot about them. Now they feared the phones may have been damaged from the fall.

"Do you think Hopalong Cassidy will come looking for us?" she asked. She could see a far off mesa by looking to her right. The slight canyon they had ridden through was off to her left. "He said that trust was the key to all of us having a happy ending."

"He'll look for us," said Hanky keeping the rest of his comments to himself; those comments dealing with, if he finds us in time. In his heart he trusted that Hopalong Cassidy was a man of his word. Then he began to doubt. When he looked up he could see large dark birds circling high above them. He didn't need his imagination to tell him the birds were buzzards contemplating how to split up an inviting meal of a brother and sister. Suddenly, Hanky started bouncing and squirming toward E Jee saying, "Do the same, E Jee. Get your hands in line with mine and make sure they can touch my rope. I'll do the same with you."

Hanky and E Jee soon saw their enthusiasm to get untied, perhaps get to their cell phones and even escape turn into frustration as the coarse ropes and clumsy knots make their fingers ache and, in Hanky's case, start to bleed. "Darn it, E Jee," he said, "Your knot isn't moving at all. I can't get it to budge." He looked up and saw that the circling buzzards had grown in numbers and appeared to be in no hurry to introduce themselves to Hanky and E Jee.

Hanky continued to struggle with E Jee's knot, his fingers turning raw and exposing nerves that stung. "Any luck," he asked E Jee. His answer was feeling his sister squirming more, a string of her favorite expressions coming from her. "Gee whiz; jeepers creepers and golly geez filled the silent desert.

"I'm trying," answered E Jee, her effort evident in her reply as she continued to squirm. Her tiny fingers dug and pecked at the large knot holding her brother's hands together, the knot feeling as if it had been glued shut. "I'm trying as hard as I can," she repeated.

Hanky's hands hurt even more and he turned his head for a moment to take another look at the circling birds. Then his head turned until his cheek was on the ground. He didn't like what he thought he saw. At first, he thought his eyes were playing tricks on him the way they did when he had landed on the ground. Then he knew his eyes weren't playing tricks on him. What he saw was moving at him. What he saw wasn't walking or hopping or circling for a landing. What he saw coming toward him was crawling and slithering. He swallowed hard. It was the biggest snake he had ever seen; bigger than what he marveled at during visits to the Lincoln Park Zoo in Chicago. Hanky hated snakes. He feared them. They scared the daylights out of him.

"Hey," shouted E Jee, "why did you move? I can't reach your ropes."

Hanky had pivoted his body so his feet were facing the large approaching snake; a Diamondback rattle snake of, to Hanky, immense proportions. Before both Hanky and the snake—E Jee had no idea of what was happening—realized what was happening, Hanky had dug his heels into the sand and started kicking for all he was worth. Sand, rock and gravel hit the snake head on, but that didn't stop him. Hanky kept kicking with every ounce of energy he could find and started screaming at the top of his voice. "Get out of here," he yelled so loud he frightened E Jee. "Go on, get! Scram! Beat it!"

The rattle snake didn't listen.

E Jee, not knowing what was going on, got annoyed with her brother asking him, "Who are you shouting at, Ding Dong?"

Hanky didn't answer her because he was having a hard enough time comprehending what he was now seeing. On the ground, next to he and E Jee were the pair of miniature boots their Grandpa Bucky had given them. Hanky suddenly remembered the one word attached to the boots; magic. The boots must have been jarred loose from their jeans when he and his sister were unceremoniously dumped off the horses.

The snake kept getting closer and Hanky kept kicking.

"Hanky, what are you doing?" asked E Jee knowing that something wasn't right. Her answer came in the form of more of her brother's grunts and screams.

What Hanky saw next would have never been believed even if he had his iPhone camera take a video. The pair of boots had gotten into position on each side of the snake's gigantic arrow shaped head.

That didn't stop Hanky from continuing to kick up a small sand storm with his own boots.

The pair of miniature boots somehow had jumped up and positioned themselves on each side of the snake's head. Hanky's own kicking seemed to freeze in midair as he watched the miniature boots launch a furious attack bludgeoning the eyes of the snake until it was twisting and lashing out at empty space. The boots didn't stop until Hanky saw the snake snap its head sending the boots hurdling to the ground. With that, the snake totally confused at what had happened to him, turned and slithered away to avoid anymore bombardment from the feet of Hanky Goodson and two unknown assailants that had tried to remove his eyes from his head. His long tongue darting in and out in apparent frustration, the snake glided away in search of a more hospitable environment and a much more easily digestible meal.

"Jeepers," said E Jee after Hanky had told her what happened, "Grandpa Bucky wasn't playing a joke on us when he said those boots were magical." She twisted and squirmed trying to get a better view of what had happened, but the snake was gone and the miniature boots were back in the same position they were when spilling out of two pockets. "Was that snake poisonous?" she asked not wanting to know the answer.

"I don't know," said Hanky. "All I know is that he was big and he was crawling right at me. Then, without wasting a breath, he said: "We better get back into position to try and unloosen those knots. I don't know how magical those boots will be if those great big birds circling over our heads decide to get friendly with us."

Unloosening the knots was easier said than done and Hanky could feel additional blisters and sores opening up on his fingers. "Any luck?" he asked his sister.

A series of grunts were her reply.

"Keep trying," he coaxed. "You can do it."

There were more grunts from her and then silence.

"You okay, E Jee," he asked. Silence was his answer. "E Jee," he said, this time louder.

"I think I got it, Hanky," she said. "I think the knot is loose."

Hanky forced his wrists to move. They wouldn't. "Are you sure?"

"I think so," said E Jee feeling the loose end of the rope in her grasp. "Let me see if I can unwind this thing."

Hanky shifted around and tried to raise his arms. They seemed to weigh a ton after having been tied up for so long. "Is it coming loose?"

"I think so, Hanky," she said as the loose end of the rope grew with her slow, painstaking unwinding, her own hands unable to move but several inches at a time. "It's moving, Hanky. I'm getting it. It's getting looser. I can feel it. Oh, Hanky, it's coming undone."

The entire process of getting the rope off of Hanky seemed to take two eternities, but Hanky was then freeing E Jee in a matter of minutes.

"Oh, I hate these ugly ropes," she said. "I never want to see them again." She tossed her rope on the ground as far away as she could. "Good riddance."

Hanky slowly coiled his rope up until it looked like it would have fit over a saddle horn. "I think you'd better do the same,

Sis," he said, nodding in the direction where her rope lay on the ground. "We might need these ropes later on."

E Jee was following her brother's instructions and slowly coiling her rope in a similar fashion he had when she asked: "How are we going to find Miss Jab's ranch from way out here?" she asked.

Hanky glanced in the direction of the small valley they had ridden through on the backs of the horses of Ringo's men. "I think we should go back in the direction where we came."

E Jee became frightened. "But, didn't that nasty Mister Ringo tell his men that they'd be going back to Miss Jab's ranch to do all kinds of bad things?"

Hanky nodded. "It's our only hope, Sis," he said trying to sound reassuring. "If we see any clouds of dust coming, we can duck into that forest of cactus looking things."

"I'm scared, Hanky."

"We'll be fine," he said trying to appear brave. "At least we got a trail to follow and that trail will lead back to Miss Jab's ranch," he said. "I'm only guessing, but I think that we were on those horses for no more than a half hour. If we start heading back now, maybe it might take us three hours or so. We might just make it back before night if all goes well for us."

"I hope so."

Hope was on their side until they saw what they had hoped they wouldn't see. "Jeepers, Hanky," do you see that?"

At first, the dust they saw on the horizon frightened them. Hanky grabbed E Jee's hand and they ran into a cluster of Organ

Pipe cacti looking for a place to hide.

"Do you think that's Ringo coming back to get us?" asked E Jee.

"I don't know," said Hanky. "He and his men took off in a different direction." He slowed down his pace and said, "Be careful of those mean looking needles on those cactus." They had sprinted about fifty yards off the trail they were following. "Come on," he said taking his sister by the hand. "No one will ever see us hiding in here. Besides, they wouldn't want to come in here anyway."

They had just entered the Organ Pipes when they saw that the source of the cloud of dust was not Ringo and his men. It was Miss Jab and she was on a buckboard being pulled by two horses. Both Hanky and E Jee bolted from their hiding place running toward the wagon that was alongside of them. They were yelling out Miss Jab's name and waving their arms for all they were worth, their coiled ropes fanning the air.

Their hearts stopped. Miss Jab kept on going. "Miss Jab!" Hanky continued to shout. "Miss Jab!"

E Jee just stood and started murmuring, repeating Miss Jab's name over and over again while trying not to cry. "Hoppy said to trust you; to trust all of us."

Then they couldn't believe what they saw next. The buckboard had come to a halt and was slowly coming back in their direction. Both Hanky and E Jee started running, several jumps being added to their strides as they could see Miss Jabs' face. She was smiling at them.

After hugs and a quick check to see that all of them were okay, Miss Jab explained that she had seen them come out of the Organ Pipes, but, because of her bad arm and knocking over her

Winchester in her excitement, it took her several minutes to grip the reins and get her team of horses under control.

Miss Jab didn't waste any time. "Climb on up here you two," she ordered gruffly. "We just might make it back to the ranch before nightfall."

Hanky and E Jee were on the buckboard bench seat in seconds, E Jee quickly positioned herself next to Miss Jab who messed up the top of her hair and said, "You can tell me all about how you got those ropes on the way back." She gave a big grin to her two passengers. "Hoppy and the boys are going to be mighty pleased when they see you." Her grin faded. "I know one person who won't be so happy to see that you two survived and I have a feeling he's in for a big surprise right about now."

Chapter 10

Ringo and his men had ridden hard, pushing their horses almost to the breaking point as they ended up at his ranch faster than he had hoped. The several extra men he had hired for an emergency had been saddled up, armed and waiting for his arrival. They were shaggy, unshaven and looked as if they had been on the trail all of their lives. Bandoleers crisscrossed their chests and they all carried repeating rifles. Each man wore a pair of six guns, the handles jutting out from worn, tattered holsters.

"You men ready to ride?" asked Ringo.

"Before I ride," one of the men started out saying, "I want to know when we're getting paid."

Ringo jerked a pistol out of his holster and shot the man right between the eyes. "Any of you men have any other questions?" he asked without looking down at the man lying motionless on the ground. He didn't wait for an answer and dug his spurs into the flanks of his horse.

The other riders followed.

Ringo thought he had a simple, surefire plan to get Miss Jab's cattle. He and his men would ride back to her ranch and take them. Hopalong Cassidy and his men would surely be tracking him to get back the two kids he had taken as hostages. "Guys like Cassidy are a bunch of saps," he had said to his men.

"They'll waste all day looking for those kids, and by that time, we'll be long gone with that herd of cattle and without that pest of a woman." He grunted out a laugh. "By the time the sun comes up tomorrow, those cattle will all be sportin' our skull and cross bones brand. Hopalong Cassidy won't be able to do a thing about it."

The rustlers rode with abandon; only one thing on each of their minds and that one thing was money; money in the form of cattle and how they were going to spend that money.

Hoppy and his men were waiting for Ringo's bunch at the ranch. The only one visible, however, was Hopalong Cassidy. He stood nonchalantly on the front porch of the ranch house looking like he was enjoying the start of an Arizona sunset, his brilliant white horse, Topper tied to the hitching rail off to the side of the front stairs. Except for the cattle in the corral, there were no other signs of life.

That should have been a red flag waving in the face of an experienced crook like Ringo. His greed, however, and the chance to finally get rid of Hopalong Cassidy totally blinded him. Had he known there were a dozen gun sights trained on him and his gang, he would have never been so bold and brazen riding up to the front porch, getting off his horse, tying him to the hitching rail and pulling out both pistols; pointing them at Hoppy.

"Fancy meeting you here, Ringo," said Hoppy in a very friendly voice.

"Likewise, Cassidy," snapped Ringo. He cocked the hammers of both pistols. "You're either a brave man, a fool or both."

"I've been called all of the above before," replied Hoppy, the tone of his voice and his posture not changing. "And, I might add, by a lot better than you."

"Flattery ain't gonna keep me from filling you full of lead, Cassidy," snarled Ringo his guns staying glued on their target, Hoppy's chest.

"I guess flattery's not going to keep your men from being aerated by my men either."

The unchanging tone of Hoppy's voice and the realization that he had ridden into a trap caused a tight feeling in Ringo's chest. The sneer on his face didn't change. His men, however, had heard Hopalong Cassidy's remark as did their horses and there was an uneasy movement from all of them.

"Oh, by the way," Hoppy added, "those men of yours you left behind when you rode off with those two young 'uns, well, I want you to know that they're safe and sound. Of course, the sheriff was more than accommodating and your boys are resting comfortably in a jail cell."

Ringo sloughed off the remark. "I can drop you to that porch in a dead heap in less than a second, Cassidy." Both of his pistols waved slowly from side to side.

"Like you dropped those two youngsters out in the desert all tied up and left to die?"

"Those snot noses gave us our getaway and now they're giving the buzzards and the coyotes a nice meal."

"Those two snot noses, by the way, are also safe and sound," said Hoppy. "Guess your boys should learn how to tie better knots. Those two snot noses, I'll have you know, were picked up by Miss Jab. They've already given the sheriff the details of what you did to them. A jury's not going to take to lightly when they hear about you and your tough guys kidnapping a couple of children. I wouldn't want to be in your boots."

As the two men played their verbal game, Hoppy's men who had been in position to surround them began to tighten their own brand of noose. Tim and Tom had been in position hidden under the front porch of the ranch house hidden by the hay bales, their weapons cocked and pointed at Ringo as he boldly, but foolishly rode up to face Hopalong Cassidy. Then, even more foolishly, he dismounted from his horse.

Gene and Roy had concealed themselves in the corral among the cattle, their guns also drawn. They had clear shots at one side of Ringo's men. The sheriff and his posse were in the barn, several in the loft. Half dozen guns were trained on the Ringo gang. Off in the distance, hiding among several giant saguaro cacti were the Lone Ranger and Tonto.

Ringo still had a sneer on his pock marked face; his several day old growth of a salt and pepper colored beard was unable to conceal the indentations and scars. No beard could ever hide his mean, ugly face.

Hoppy's eyes stayed zeroed in on Ringo's. On the one hand he knew he had Ringo all but handed over to the sheriff. On the other, however, something didn't seem totally right. Had he forgotten something; overlooked a crucial detail or forgot to count all of the cards in the deck Ringo had laid on the table. He counted the number of men in Ringo's party. There were only half a dozen or so. That was a half a dozen or so that he could see. There were a series of high hills on three sides of Miss Jab's ranch. Two of the hills were off to each side. The middle hill was in the back of the house, out of sight to Hoppy. Then it dawned on Hoppy. Ringo had men hidden in the hills just waiting for a signal of some kind to swoop down and start shooting, causing enough commotion for Ringo to open up the gate or even pull down part of the fence of the corral. With all the noise of guns going off the cattle would surely stampede.

Hoppy knew his men were watching him and that if there was any move on his part other than what he had discussed with them they should come out from their cover and round up Ringo and the prospective rustlers, hopefully without a shot. As if he were going to take a stroll around the corral, Hoppy started down the stairs, his hands nowhere near his guns.

The move surprised Ringo. In a lapse of judgment he raised one of his guns and fired it into the air. That was a signal no one expected at that point; not Hoppy's men and not Ringo's. The men on horseback hiding just behind the top of the hills were the only one's waiting for a signal. When they heard the shot their horses broke into a full gallop and came out of hiding and charged down the hill.

When Hoppy's men saw and heard the shot, they reacted as well. The barn and hayloft doors almost flew off the hinges as the sheriff and his posse rode out. Hoppy had said no gun play, but that was before Ringo fired a second shot. That one was aimed at Hoppy but only kicked up dust several feet behind Hoppy's boots as he dove under the corral fence and got lost among the shuffling legs of cattle who also heard the shots. They were startled and in no mood to stay penned up in a corral.

As Ringo's hired gun slingers galloped down the hill behind the house, several of the sheriff's posse had immobilized a small group of Ringo's men who were watching the scene between Ringo and Hoppy unfold. They only had the opportunity to turn and look, their guns never having the chance to be drawn. More guns were pointed at them than they ever knew existed. They were bound up with ropes tighter than Hanky and E Jee could have imagined.

Several more gunshots came from Ringo's band. They were answered by two shots coming from Tim and Tom. Both of Ringo's sidekicks who had been next to him were on the ground clutching at their right boots. They were the same boots that were minus the heals from the earlier shoot out. Both men would soon discover that they would find future walking difficult since their big toes had been shot off thanks to the marksmanship of Tim and Tom.

Seeing his chance, Ringo spun around, took several quick strides and jumped on his horse. He swung his black horse around and started out on the same road he and his men had used earlier when they abducted Hanky and E Jee. A second time was one too many. Coming out of the Organ Pipes at full gallop was Tonto and the Lone Ranger, the Lone Ranger shouting: "Hi-ho, Silver!"

Ringo spurred his horse and turned him in the direction of the barn. As he did so he reached into the open flap of his saddle bag and pulled out a cylinder shape container about a foot long. It was several sticks of dynamite banded together, a short fuse hanging down from the top. His other hand reached in the pocket of his shirt and pulled out a wooden stick match. There was a swipe of the match across his rough jeans and the dynamite fuse began to smoke and hiss. As his horse neared the open barn he gave the dynamite a mighty toss with all of his strength. The dynamite landed in the hay loft where Hanky and E Jee had been ordered to stay put by Hoppy until Ringo and his men had been arrested by the sheriff. They had done what they had been told to do. What they hadn't been told to do was how to react with several sticks of dynamite lying at their feet, a fuse smoldering and smoking.

The other men from the posse who had been in the hayloft had swung down to the ground floor when the shooting had started. They had their weapons pointed at Ringo.

The bully and coward had no place to run and his chance for escape came to an end as he looked into a rather extra long barrel of a pistol held by the tall, sullen sheriff.

Ringo's men cleared the hill they had raced down, their guns spitting out fire, most of the bullets hitting the ranch house, some of the others being buried in the barn walls and the rest dropping to the desert sand once their energy had been spent. That's when Gene and Roy appeared from the corral and Tim and Tom kicked away the bales of hay from the front porch. At the same time, Tonto and the Lone Ranger road up behind Ringo's men. With a corral full of cattle in front of them and armed men on the other three sides, they had no place to ride. The great cattle rustle was over.

That's what everyone including Hoppy thought as he crawled out from under the corral fence, brushed himself off and headed for where the sheriff had Ringo. He had only taken one step when the dynamite went off blowing the top front of Miss Jab's hay loft into smithereens. Shattered boards sailed everywhere as the blast sent the cattle charging into the corral fence on one side. Surprisingly, the fence held and the pent up energy of the cattle had them moving in a large circle within the corral.

Miss Jab's had been watching the showdown unfold from a safe position from behind the barn. She had obeyed Hoppy's wishes for her to keep out of the fray even though she had ached to use her guns. Her ache had become painful especially after she had recognized one of the men on a palomino next to Ringo as her former ranch hand, Moon. She felt her heart sink when she heard the explosion and part of the barn rained down on her. She jumped off her buckboard and headed for inside the barn. She had only one thing on her mind and that one thing was the safety and well being of Hanky and E Jee. She saw what the explosion did to her barn, but that didn't matter to her. Hanky and E Jee were in the hayloft staying out of sight like they had been told. Now they were still out of sight.

Chapter 11

In a split second before the dynamite turned the hay loft into a charred, splintered disaster, Hanky had shoved his sister toward a stack of hay bales. He had shoved her so hard she sailed over the top of the bales with Hanky's momentum carrying him over the top with her. Hanky's feet caught the top bales and they came crashing down on him and E Jee. Then they heard the explosion and their worlds went black.

Neither Hanky nor E Jee knew how long they had been buried under hay and loose boards. It was Hanky who felt a hand on his shoulder and he heard a man's voice.

"Hey, kid, you okay?" the voice asked.

"I think so," said Hanky slowly, his voice groggy. He couldn't comprehend where he was at and why a male voice, one that was new and strange on the one hand, but familiar on the other, was asking him if he were okay.

"Stay put and we'll get you out," said the male voice.

Hanky thought for a minute. "Yeah, sure," he repeated still not understanding where he was at and why he needed help. Then he remembered hearing a loud noise and a crash. That was the last thing he remembered. Then he thought of his sister. "E

Jee," he shouted out, as he struggled against the crushing weight pressing down on him. "E Jee," he yelled again!

"Easy, kid," the male voice said his two short words followed by a series of grunts and the noise of what sounded like wood being tossed on a pile. "Your sister's fine. She's with your parents." There were more sounds of wood being tossed into piles. The tossing was accompanied by several other voices shouting out instructions, warning to be careful being heard by Hanky. "Careful of what," he thought. Then he hollered out his sister's name again.

"Your sister's fine, kid," came a reply.

"E Jee's fine," said Hanky feeling both relieved and confused. Then the totality of the man's words hit him. "She's with Mom and Dad?"

Wooden debris continued to crash around Hanky, but he could feel the once crushing weight on him disappearing. Then he could see his legs, his jeans covered with dirt and dust. He tried to move them and they moved. His hands and arms began to push and shove at the weight pinning him down. In a moment he could feel himself able to slide, "Mom and Dad," he repeated, his excitement growing. "Oh, wow," he yelled out as if opening a birthday present, the gift something he had dreamed about. "Wait until Grandpa Bucky hears about Hoppy." Then he felt a pair of hands grab him under the arms and he felt himself being pulled out from under the rubble that had him pinned down.

"Easy does it, kid," he heard the same man's voice say. "You're almost free."

Then he was free. Excited, he rolled over and got to his hands and knees. The he looked up and couldn't believe what he saw. "You," he said.

"The one and only," the man said. He places both hands on Hanky's shoulders. "You sure you're okay?" he asked.

"I think so," replied Hanky not knowing what else to say and too confused to say anything else.

"You hurtin' anywhere?" the man asked. "Anything feel broken?"

Hanky's head went slowly from side to side several times. He didn't say a word only kept kneeling and looking at the man. Then he finally said: "You're the guy E Jee and I saw sitting at a table in a private office. You're one of the guys who shows people around that museum that's filled with the Hopalong Cassidy stuff."

"Guilty on all counts," the man said as he stood in front of Hanky offering his hands to help Hanky stand.

"You're the guy who pushed us through that black curtain and out into the desert where we almost got killed by Ringo and his gang."

The man slowly pulled Hanky to his feet. "Not guilty about pushing you and having you almost get killed by this Ringo person you just mentioned," said the man who was indeed one of the museum's tour guides. "When I told you and your sister you had to leave my private room the both of you high-tailed out of there like a couple of scared rabbits. Do you remember that?"

Hanky's head went up and down once, not sure of what he remembered while his eyes staying glued to the man.

"The problem is you two kids thought that black velvet curtain was an exit door," he said seriously. "It wasn't."

"It wasn't?" asked Hanky.

"Well, it was and it wasn't," said the man. "You and your sister did go through a door, but it was the door to part of an old movie set that was once used in a Hopalong Cassidy movie way back before you were born. You and your sister knocked the entire gosh darn thing down and got buried under the rubble. We had a devil of a time getting you out."

"There were others?" asked Hanky feeling foolish.

"Heck," the man started out as he checked Hanky for any possible injuries, "I had your parents and those other people, your grandparents and that couple down the road that own the motel were in here in a heartbeat. You and your sister had us all scared to death."

"I'm sorry," said Hanky softly. He wanted to cry, but fought back the tears. "You say E Jee's okay."

"She's just fine," replied the man. "We heard her almost immediately. She was yelling something about a person named, Miss Jab. Kept repeating the name over and over, asking this Miss Jab person to save her." He paused and gave Hanky a strange look. "She was asking to be saved from a person named Ringo. That was the same name you just used." He bent over and looked into Hanky's eyes. "You sure you didn't get knocked on the head or something?"

"I'm fine," said Hanky. Then he noticed that the man's western shirt was torn and stained with dirt and, at the area of the shoulder in the same exact spot where Miss Jab had been shot, was what looked like fresh blood. "Are you okay, Sir?" he asked nodding at the red stain on the man's shirt sleeve.

"Oh, that's nothin'," he said. "Caught it on a nail or screw or something sharp when I was pulling your sister out from under that mess you two made. I'll take care of it as soon as we get you back with your parents."

Hanky's mother was the first to greet him when he emerged from the private office with the tour guide. She was hugging him, loving him and scolding him all at the same time. "Are you hurt?" she asked, adding, "What were you and your sister thinking about by trespassing into that man's private quarters?"

"But, Mom," pleaded Hanky, "we didn't do anything wrong. Honest we didn't. I swear."

He never got to finish. "Don't you but your mother, Henry John Goodson," his father said as he put a gentle hand on the shoulder of his son's soiled shirt. "Are you sure you're okay," he quickly asked.

Hanky nodded then saw his Grandpa Bucky walking slowly toward him. There was a look on his face that Hanky had never experienced before and he wasn't sure he wanted to now.

"Had quite an adventure now, did you," Grandpa Bucky said, his eyes smiling but not the rest of his face. "Your sister told me after she calmed down." He pursed his lips then said: "So you two met Hopalong Cassidy and this Miss Jab lady and a whole ranch in Arizona loaded with cowboys who you thought you recognized?" His head went up and down several times. "And then some mean old man with an ugly, scary face tied the both of you up and dropped you in the middle of the desert where buzzards and a rattle snake almost got you. Is that right?"

"Kind of, Grandpa," said Hanky, his reply almost in a whisper so the others wouldn't hear him. He knew they thought what he and his sister had said had been made up; that they used the story to cover up the accident they caused by knocking over the old movie set. "Grandpa," he said, tears suddenly spilling down his cheeks, "we really met Hoppy. And there was this lady, Miss Jab; she could out shoot most men. Hoppy said so." Hanky barely had time to breathe. "Miss Jab, well, she helped us when we thought we were lost in the desert, and there was a man named, Ringo who wanted to kill us and steal Miss Jab's cattle." His words were flying out of him. "And there were all of these cowboys who all looked like cowboys I had seen before. You know, like the cowboy actors in that set of compact disks in all of those old black and white western movies you gave E Jee and me last Christmas." He was on a roll. "We watched every one of them, some two or three times."

His grandfather barely nodded.

"And, Grandpa," added Hanky. "You know those tiny cowboy boots you gave us, the ones that you said were magic?" He paused and swallowed hard. "They were, Grandpa. They saved our lives."

"Well, Hanky," his grandfather said to him, "I'm glad you and E Jee liked those old movies." His eyes traveled up and down Hanky. "And, I'm sure glad you didn't get hurt in that accident with the movie set. Are you two sure you're oaky?"

"I'm sure, Grandpa." He saw his grandmother coming toward him. She was holding E Jee's hand. "And I never doubted you one second about those tiny boots being magical. No, Sir, not one second."

"Hi, Hanky," said a shaken but relieved looking E Jee. "I'm glad you weren't hurt."

"Me too," said Hanky, his fists rubbing at his eyes for a moment. "You okay?"

"I'm fine too," she said. "Are you sure you're okay?"

He head went up and down once.

"You saved my life from that bad old Ringo's dynamite," she whispered.

Her whisper wasn't soft enough. "Now no more about cattle rustlers and cowboys trying to kill you," E Jee's grandmother warned. "Mister Mushy and his wife have planned a big barbeque for us tonight back at the motel and that includes using the swimming pool." She paused and looked at her two grandchildren. "And neither of you will mention Hopalong Cassidy tonight," she warned. "Do you both understand?"

E Jee and Hanky looked at one another, smiled and shook their heads up and down.

Chapter 12

The barbeque and pool party had been fun for everyone. Mister Mushy had showed off his skill on the grill with his St. Louis cut pork ribs and, a first for the family except Grandpa and Grandma Goodson, his Italian potato salad and Fettuccini Alfredo.

Hanky and E Jee ate as if they hadn't seen food in a week. They almost drowned themselves in the countless cans of soft drinks they plucked from a round wash tub that was covered with a mound of chipped ice. Then they nearly drowned themselves in the pool by doing what they thought were creative dives off the diving board with a too slick surface. E Jee had been in the water after her impersonation of a cannon ball when Hanky was going to do a front flip. He had never done one before. He didn't this time. His feet hit a wet spot on the board and he went airborne, his arms and legs going in different directions before landing inches from E Jee who was kicking herself away from being landed on. She ended up kicking Hanky.

Too much food and drink sent Donald and Marie Goodson off to their room with their children following close behind. There were no complaints from Hanky and E Jee about going to bed. Beside their harrowing experience in the Arizona desert with Hoppy and Miss Jab, that evening they enjoyed feeling more a part of what a family means than ever before. Full stomachs and frolicking in the pool with everyone except their Gram Gini who hated to get chlorine in her hair and Mister Mushy's wife, who said she always broke out in white blotches after she had used the pool, had drained every ounce of energy from the twins' batteries. The last words out of them when their heads hit their pillow had to do with Hopalong Cassidy, Hanky saying to his sister: "I can't wait until we get back home so we can go over to Grandpa Bucky's and tell him what we really saw."

E Jee let out a yawn that made her sound as if she were already sleeping. "I can't wait to show Grandpa Bucky the pictures I took with my phone." Her last words to her brother were: "I really miss that ranch and Miss Jab. She was a nice lady."

It was the grandparents and old friends who sat up well into the night reminiscing about the days when they were kids like the grandchildren. The conversation eventually switched to the booing of Hopalong Cassidy at the circus and Grandpa Bucky trying to jokingly pass the blame onto his friend, Mushy, who everyone knew wasn't even at the circus.

"It's a wonder you two are still friends after all these years," said Mushy's wife adding to the conversation even though she had made the same remark over the years on the rare occasions when the friends got together.

"Ha," laughed Grandpa Bucky. "Back then a guy did what a guy had to do to save his backside from getting a wallop."

Mushy was grinning. "What old Bucky isn't telling you is that I ratted on him for things he didn't do just so I could save my own skin."

"Now that's what I call genuine friendship," said Mushy's

wife.

"I agree," said Gram Gini.

"How come you never did tell us who did the booing at the circus?" Mushy asked.

Grandpa Bucky didn't wait a second. "The Code, Mushy," he said. "It was our Code."

Mushy's grin turned to an exploding laugh. "Ah, the Code," he said. He thought for a moment then said to Bucky: "All of those nuns have got to be dead by now. So are the priests. Come on, Bucky, fess up and tell us that you're the one who did it."

Bucky made a cross over his heart. "It wasn't me."

"But you darn well know who did it, don't you?" said Mushy.

"Bucky smiled.

"Well, darn it, Bucky, tell us."

Bucky sat silent, smiling and thinking.

"Are you or aren't you?" Mushy asked, pushing ahead.

The wives leaned forward in their poolside chairs, waiting; listening.

"Well," said Bucky.

Chapter 13

The ride back to Chicago was every bit as hot and humid as going to Ohio; uncomfortable border line agony filling the van even at seventy miles per hour. The only difference from going to coming was that Hanky and E Jee didn't feel the hot summer wind blowing through the van. They sat in back as usual only this time things weren't as usual. There was no fighting, no arguing; one sibling didn't tease the other. Every word out of them was in a whisper. At times, their parents and grandparents thought they were sleeping. Their parents and grandmother found themselves dozing through Ohio and Indiana; their grandmother and mother waking up long enough to order Grandpa Bucky to stop for a bathroom break and get cold drinks.

Hanky and E Jee didn't talk much about their experiences with Hoppy, Miss Jab, Ringo and the ranch. Their discussion was centered on the supporting cast of cowboys they had encountered and who had befriended them; even saving their lives.

"I knew I saw those guys before," said Hanky in E Jee's ear. "I knew every one of them."

"I did too," whispered E Jee back to her brother. "They were all in those DVD's grandpa gave us for Christmas."

"I know," said Hanky agreeing with his sister for one of the rare times in their lives. "They were old movie stars from those ancient black and white cowboy movies."

"Geez, and they looked just like they did in those movies we watched so many times," said E Jee, her lips almost touching Hanky's ear. "I thought I recognized that guy they called Randy right from the start," she said. "I thought he was kind of a hunk the first time I saw him a movie.

"That wasn't a Randy, but Randolph Scott," said Hanky, his voice a little louder and showing excitement. "He made a lot of western movies. Not as many as Hopalong Cassidy, but he made a bunch."

They stopped talking when they saw their mother's head turn and look into the back of the van. "I thought you two were asleep," she said.

"We were, Mom," said Hanky, "but Miss Pest here kept leaning against me. It's too hot to have anyone lean against you."

"I agree," said his mother before turning back.

"Thanks for blaming me," said E Jee, her voice in a hush. "Do you know who else I recognized right away?" she said sounding eager to tell her brother. "That old guy with the shaggy beard they called Chats."

"I know," whispered Hanky back. "That was Gabby Hayes."

"Kind of spooky if you ask me," E Jee continued. "Even spookier were those two guys, Tim and Tom. I couldn't remember their names until you told me."

"Tom Mix was easy," said Hanky. "But that guy, Tim Holt, well, he wasn't as famous or popular. One guy I thought should have been in that group was that cowboy who was always fighting. You know the one I mean. His hat never came off no matter how many punches he threw. Bob Steele was his name.

Grandpa Bucky called him a little fart who needed a ladder to mount up on his horse."

E Jee giggled.

The sat in silence not noticing the sweltering heat until Hanky turned to E Jee and asked: "That guy who was the tall sheriff really stunned me when I saw him."

"Me too," said E Jee.

"He wasn't in any of those old movies Grandpa Bucky gave to us."

"I didn't remember him in any of those either," said E Jee. "I almost fell over when you told me. Geez, that sheriff was Gary Cooper."

"Yeah, he was one of the old guys, but not as old as some of the others. They were ancient."

The heat finally got to both Hanky and E Jee with E Jee falling asleep first. Hanky's head kept bouncing up and down as he fought going to sleep. There was something gnawing on his mind and it was driving him crazy until he realized that he hadn't checked on his good luck charm.

Chapter 14

Hanky and E Jee took their usual short cut through the neighbor's gangways and yards to the side entrance of their Grandpa Bucky's house where they stood waiting for someone to answer the door.

"Whadda you two want?" came the familiar gruff voice from behind the open door; Grandpa Bucky not visible. "Didn't think you two would bother coming over any more since bein' out in Arizona with Hoppy blowin' up barns." The door opened more. "Well, whadda you waitin' for?" the voice of their grandfather asked, "an engraved invitation from the White House?" There was the familiar laugh. "Maybe you want one from the Hopalong Cassidy Museum in Ohio." The door opened wide and Grandpa Bucky poked his unshaven face around the edge of the door. "Maybe from Hoppy himself 'cause you two are already on a first name basis with him."

"You ain't funny, Grandpa," said Hanky. "You and that Hoppy museum and that friend of yours, Mister Mushy aren't funny either," he continued as he walked into the side entrance, stopping at the steps leading up to the den. E Jee was right behind him.

"Gee whiz, Grandpa," she said as she walked in looking up into her grandfather's droopy, smiling red lined eyes. "You shouldn't have done that to us."

"I didn't do a thing," their grandfather said as he ushered in his two grandchildren and nodded up the stairs. "Your imaginations did it all." He paused and looked at them both. "That, and you're not being able to read a simple one word sign," he said. He let out a sigh and said, "Private."

"We didn't imagine any of that stuff, Grandpa," said Hanky trying to be respectful, the memory of being tied up and left to die out in the Arizona desert still very vivid.

"Okay, okay, everything that happened in Ohio was real," he said. "Now, I take it that you two didn't stop by for a cup of tea." He nodded again toward the door leading to the attic stairs and his den. "Okay, get the lead out of your underwear and up you go."

They sat where they always did; Grandpa Bucky in his worn lounger chair and Hanky and E Jee on the floor, legs curled up, at their grandfather's feet.

Hanky didn't give his grandfather a chance to say another word. "Okay, Grandpa," he said, startling the old man and E Jee. "Fess up," he continued staring at his grandfather. "Did you boo Hopalong Cassidy?"

Grandpa Bucky sat staring off into space as if he were in another time and place. He didn't say a word for well over, what seemed to his grandchildren, a very long and uncomfortable minute. "I told you I didn't," he said slowly to his grandson. "And, I didn't; pure and simple."

"But, Hoppy said he heard the boo," said Hanky leaning forward. "I heard him say so."

"Geez, Grandpa, I did too," said E Jee being polite.

"So did I," said Grandpa Bucky softly. "Didn't you two listen to me the last time you were here when I told you I didn't, but I knew who did?"

"Yeah, Grandpa," said Hanky, "but Hoppy seemed to think it was you."

"He did, Grandpa," said E Jee respectfully.

"I don't know what you two heard while visiting that museum, but the only time I saw the real Hopalong Cassidy was at the circus when I was your age. You know all that."

Two heads shook in understanding.

"I also told you that I knew who did it, didn't I?"

Two heads continued to nod. "We know that, Grandpa," interjected Hanky. "We know that Mister Mushy didn't do it because he wasn't there."

"Right you are, Hanky," said Grandpa Bucky a smile beginning to form. "And you say that old Hoppy said he heard that boo and he said I did it." He pointed at himself. "He heard me, Joseph Arlen Bucky Goodson boo him?"

Both Hanky and E Jee thought for a minute until Hanky said: "Well, Grandpa, he didn't actually say it was you, but E Jee and I could see he was thinking real hard about it."

"Thinking real hard," repeated Grandpa Bucky. "Boy, if that don't sound like my name being stated by Hopalong Cassidy, then I guess I'm guilty." He paused. "Of course, Hoppy didn't say my name and why would he?" His pause was extra long as his eyes traveled back and forth several times. "He didn't say it because I didn't do it," he said putting emphasis on the final period. He looked extremely satisfied as he said to his grandchildren: "Now show me all those pictures of Hoppy and all of those characters you met while shootin' up the old west."

E Jee was the first to have her iPhone out. "You swipe your finger across the screen like this when you want to see another picture," she said, demonstrating the technique to her grandfather.

Grandpa Bucky gave a low grunt.

After E Jee's pictures had been exhausted, Hanky handed over his camera to him. "You do the same thing, Grandpa," he said politely giving his index finger a wave.

Both Hanky and E Jee watched their grandfather as he seemed to study each picture, his eyes never looking up. A couple of times he repeated an old cowboy movie star's name, but the twins never saw a change in his facial expressions.

"Interesting," said Grandpa Bucky handing Hanky his phone after he was finished. He pushed back in his lounger as far as it would go and folded his hands across his stomach. "Interesting," he said again, then didn't say a word.

Hanky and E Jee didn't know what to do. Their grandfather had never been without a word, kind or otherwise, since they had started coming up to his den. E Jee felt uneasy and scooted forward until her head was resting on the foot rest of the lounger. "Grandpa," she said softly, "did we do something wrong?"

Their grandfather raised his head and they could see tears in his eyes. They didn't say a word.

"Not too long ago, your grandmother and I went to a wake and funeral of a dear friend," he started out staying almost motionless. "He was my very best friend in the entire world. They didn't come any better than him. We were best pals in grammar school; ran together constantly and were always being yelled at by the nuns at school and our parents." His head went slowly from side to side and the tears began to slowly run down his lined cheeks. We stayed friends forever, always there for one another, even when we were raising our own families and watching them get married." He dabbed at his eyes with the upturned cuffs of his shirt sleeves.

Hanky and E Jee sat not knowing what to say. They had never seen their grandfather cry before. To them, grandfathers weren't supposed to cry. They were the leaders of families.

"I will never forget Tommy Fox," he said. He added an emphatic, "Never."

"Jeepers creepers, Grandpa," said E Jee, was your best friend the one who booed Hopalong Cassidy at the circus?"

"Yeah, Grandpa," chimed in Hanky. "Are you protecting your buddy because of that code of yours you once told us about?"

Grandpa Bucky sat up in his lounger, leaned forward and wiped his eyes dry. "By golly," he said, the smile returning. "You two do know how to listen after all. And, here I thought I had a couple of mentally impaired grandchildren."

"Oh, Grandpa, gee willickers, you know better than that," said E Jee getting to her knees.

Hanky was also on his knees. "It was your best pal, Tommy Fox who booed Hoppy at the circus, wasn't it?" he said leaning forward, the palms of his hands resting on the worn area rug in front of his grandfather. "Come on, Grandpa, you can tell us."

"Geez, Grandpa, come on tell us."

Grandpa Bucky leaned forward in his chair and looked lovingly at his two grandchildren. "What kind of a best pal would I be if I snitched and violated the Code?"

"You'd still be a best pal," said Hanky trying his best to coax his grandfather to telling who booed Hopalong Cassidy."

"Sure you would, Grandpa."

"Grandpa Bucky let out a sigh. "Hoppy was a great man and Tommy and I thought he was the best. But, there were some things that were better than Hopalong Cassidy back then. Two of those things were the Code and having a best pal."

"Okay, so tell us," said Hanky, his arms outstretched as if coaxing his grandfather.

"Grandpa," hollered E Jee.

"Well, I will tell you this."

Their grandfather leaned forward in his longer and said: "If you really want to know about Hopalong Cassidy, you get on those electronic contraptions of yours and check out a fellow by the name of McClain. He wrote a song way back when your grandfather was a lot younger." He smiled, "I think your grandmother was known as a Flower Child back then.

The twins looked puzzled.

"Check out Miss American Pie," he said grinning. "Then I'll tell you."

Epilogue

The twins had walked slowly and quietly back to their house. For the first time ever they didn't say a word. There wasn't even a, goodbye from them to either of their grandparents. When they got home they merely muttered, "Hi," to their mother before disappearing into the bedroom they shared, the room also where they had twin study desks and their computer that they fought over when assignments were due the next day.

Hanky flopped down on his perfectly made bed, a definite taboo set down by his mother, and said: "What's with Grandpa Bucky and his old music?"

"I don't know," replied E Jee as she turned on their desk top computer. "But I'm going to find out one way or another who booed Hopalong Cassidy."

"How you gonna do that, Sis?" Hanky asked, then answering his own question. "By listening to some old song about an 'American Pie'?"

Author's Note:
Check out Google for the 1971 Copyrighted poem by Don McClean to Hopalong Cassidy.

--Dick Baran

A Mouse Gate Adventure Book
What's your adventure?
www.mousegate.com

Title: Where Have All the Go-Go's Gone?

Part I

- Author: Richard Baran
- Publisher: TotalRecall Publications, Inc.
- Hard Cover, ISBN: 9781590952399
- Paperback, ISBN: 9781590952405
- Ebook, Nook, Kindle, ISBN: 9781590952412
- Number of pages: 304
- Publication Date: 2015

Bo Pepperwall's intelligence dwarfed Mensa's parameters. He was perceived as strange thereby resulting in his being ridiculed by many, shunned by most and being called, Bo the Schmoe by all. Then he faced a dilemma. He had to choose between money (which he never had) and morals (which he also lacked). Should he weasel a part of his recently widowed sister's inheritance for a business venture or should he turn in the killer of her husband, his despicable brother-in-law? He chooses both. Bo opens La Tinkerbelle's a Go-Go, a 1960's retro discotheque in an abandoned factory building in a Chicago slum using a theme from the legend of Peter Pan. Surrounding himself with bizarre employees (each having a unique vision of reality) who put fun into dysfunctional, his dream nearly goes bust. Then a Chicago gossip columnist prints a story that has customers lined up and Bo collides with his dilemma. The collision buries him in money and public adulation. Success, however, can't cover his moral guilt in the surprise ending to this murder mystery farce that is more farce than mystery.

Title: When Will They Ever Learn?

Part II Where Have All the Go-Go's Gone?

- Author: Richard Baran
- Publisher: TotalRecall Publications, Inc.
- Hard Cover, ISBN: 9781590952429
- Paperback, ISBN: 9781590952436
- Ebook, Nook, Kindle, ISBN: 9781590952443
- Number of pages: 220
- Publication Date: 2015

Bo Pepperwall, a card carrying member of Mensa, dreamer, conniver and ridiculed lifelong loser opens *La Tinkerbelle's a Go-Go*. A 1960's retro discotheque located in a Chicago slum, he uses a theme from the legend of Peter Pan that includes a scantily clad Tinker Bell. He finances his business by weaseling part of his sister's inheritance away from her. He also witnesses the murder of his despicable brother-in-law, the mayor of Glen Forest on the Watercourse, a prestigious Chicago North Shore community. Bo, however, remains a loser and his garish disco faces bankruptcy until an article by a Chicago gossip columnist turns it into a bonanza. That same day, Tinker Bell's outraged mother accidentally sets fire to La Tinkerbelle's and destroys the booming business. Bo and his employees—along with two black cats named Heckle and Jeckle—end up in court charged with violations of the Mann Act; contributing to the delinquency of minors; ignoring EPA laws; cruelty to animals and presenting lewd and indecent performances. Bo turns in the killer and the court finds him innocent of the criminal charges in the surprise ending to this murder mystery zany comedy.

Title: The Jacket

- Author: Richard Baran
- Publisher: TotalRecall Publications, Inc.
- Hard Cover ISBN: 9781590955659
- Paperback, ISBN: 9781590955666
- Ebook, Nook, Kindle, ISBN: 9781590955673
- Number of pages: 352
- Publication Date: 2013

Tidge Mackiewicz, new patriarch of his family, received several orders from his dying father, Kid Scream. One order stated that Tidge should quit believing in Santa Claus and stop acting like every day was Christmas. Tidge should also abandon his belief that the Luftwaffe shot down Santa Claus on Christmas Eve in 1944 and Santa survived.

Title: Heroes and Idles

- Author: Richard Baran
- Publisher: TotalRecall Publications, Inc.
- Paperback, ISBN:
- Ebook, Nook, Kindle, ISBN:
- Number of pages: 186
- Publication Date: 2016

A burlesque star, Indian Chief, two cantankerous grandfathers, an Italian grandmother who drinks whiskey from a Mason jar, a Prussian officer and a Chicago Cub baseball star impact four young lives.

Tess, Stan, Georgie and Gil had their idols. Tess worshipped her World War II era burlesque star, Aunt Rose and an Ojibwa Indian Chief, John Proud Bear in *Lunch with a Gypsy*. Georgie, a young father entangled in an affair, drew guidance from his immigrant Italian grandmother, Nana Beam's whiskey induced lessons about repentance in *I've Got a Secret*. Stan idolized his two cantankerous grandfathers and their lesson he learned about the real world. It was the death of his wife and then his mother that led him back to his high school sweetheart from four decades ago in *The One that Got Away*. Thirteen year old Gil had three heroes. His Poppy Paul taught him to respect his given name, Gilead. Gil's father formally introduced him to Wrigley Field the day after the Chicago Cubs traded Gil's third idol, Andy Pafko to the Brooklyn Dodgers. Tragically, death claimed Gil's father soon after and Gil later found a unique way to keep his dad's memory alive in *Trading Prushka*.

Title: The Dutchman's Gift

- Author: Richard Baran
- Publisher: TotalRecall Publications, Inc.
- Paperback, ISBN: 9781590952979
- Ebook, Nook, Kindle, ISBN: 9781590952986
- Number of pages: 124
- Publication Date: 2015

A twelve year old boy finds a magical Apache arrowhead while hiking with his grandfather in the Superstition Mountains of Arizona. The arrowhead transports the boy from a Disney World rollercoaster ride back over one hundred and fifty years to the Superstitions where he meets "The Lost Dutchman."

Title: Shutter Bug

- Author: Richard Baran
- Publisher: TotalRecall Publications, Inc.
- Paperback, ISBN: 9781590953167
- Ebook, Nook, Kindle, ISBN: 9781590953174
- Number of pages: 176
- Publication Date: 2016

Emma Grace Waveland, a self-proclaimed Shutter Bug at twelve, finds herself transported from a safari in Disney World to Africa's Serengeti where she joins a group of professional hunters who capture wild animals for zoos. Her new adventure brings her face-to-face with deadly crocodiles, a giant rhino, a python, a lady photographer who looks like a young version of her great grandmother, hunters who resemble old movie stars and a camp cook with mysterious powers. Her family doesn't believe her when she returns from her trip, but she has evidence on her cameras' memory cards and her iPhone.

www.ingramcontent.com/pod-product-compliance
Lightning Source LLC
Chambersburg PA
CBHW030207130726
47898CB00012B/916